HAMISH HAMILTON

THE EMPTY SPACE

Geetanjali Shree is the author of five novels and five short story collections. Her works have been translated into English, French, German, Serbian and in several Indian languages. They have received multiple national and international awards including the 2022 International Booker Prize. She lives in New Delhi.

Nivedita Menon teaches political thought at Jawaharlal Nehru University, Delhi. Her previous books include *Recovering Subversion: Feminist Politics Beyond the Law* (2004), *Sexualities*, an edited volume (2007) and *Power and Contestation: India after 1989* (2007, co-authored with Aditya Nigam). An active commentator on the blog kafila.org, she has also translated fiction and non-fiction from Hindi and Malayalam into English. She has been active with citizens' forums in Delhi on secularism, workers' and women's rights, sexuality, and in opposition to the nuclear bomb.

35 INDIA

Celebrating 35 Years of
Penguin Random House India

PRAISE FOR THE BOOK

'Geetanjali Shree's passionate tale of loss, love and victimhood, in a world of ubiquitous terror, is an immersive journey into the hearts of women and men haunted by sorrow and guilt. It is a swift-moving story, seamlessly translated from the Hindi, that draws you deep into the eerie empty spaces of existence'—Paul Zacharia

'*The Empty Space* by Geetanjali Shree, translated by Nivedita Menon, provides a thrilling window to the very best of contemporary literature from the subcontinent; this fragmentary Hindi bildungsroman about the aftermath of a suicide bombing is truly outstanding'—Jacques Testard

'*The Empty Space* attempts to personalize a terrorist attack and poignantly steers the reader to grapple with the terrible destruction after a bomb blast'—*Sunday Guardian*

THE EMPTY SPACE

GEETANJALI SHREE

Translated from the Hindi by
NIVEDITA MENON

PENGUIN
An imprint of Penguin Random House

HAMISH HAMILTON

USA | Canada | UK | Ireland | Australia
New Zealand | India | South Africa | China

Hamish Hamilton is part of the Penguin Random House group of companies whose addresses can be found at global.penguinrandomhouse.com

Published by Penguin Random House India Pvt. Ltd
4th Floor, Capital Tower 1, MG Road,
Gurugram 122 002, Haryana, India

Penguin Random House India

First published in Hindi as *Khali Jagah* by Rajkamal Prakashan 2006
First published in English in Harper Perennial by HarperCollins Publishers India 2011
Published in Hamish Hamilton by Penguin Random House India 2023

10 9 8 7 6 5 4 3 2 1

ISBN 9780670098095

For sale in the Indian Subcontinent only

Typeset in Adobe Caslon Pro by Manipal Technologies Limited, Manipal
Printed at Thomson Press India Ltd, New Delhi

www.penguin.co.in

FSC MIX Paper FSC® C010615

To Nevenka,
in memory of Norman and David.

I would like to thank the French Cultural Centre, whose Writers-in-Residence programme enabled me to work on this novel.

1

Perhaps it was then.

When the bomb exploded.

When the bomb exploded and we scattered to pieces. It was then the moment froze in time, and we, in it. Ashes, fire, flesh. Fans, gulab jamun, pav-bhaji, idli, vada, all whirling in the air, like an argument gone astray in the cosmos.

You know how cafes are these days. You get everything everywhere now. Idli-vada in the North, pav-bhaji in the East. As *for* bombs—anywhere, at any time.

In that cafe, though, it was the very first time. The university cafe. Poor thing, in a 'safe area'. Until that moment, anyway. Buzzing with young boys and girls, admission forms clutched in their hands, fresh new meetings, '*where are you from*?' Uncertain, filled with hope. Nervousness, eating, drinking, movement, life.

Just one empty space, the size of a three-year-old. That three-year-old, myself.

I remember. I really do, believe it or not.

I remember as if it was me stuffed into the sack that held the bomb. It bursts, scatters, and out I fall, exactly into that space just right for a child my size. A perfect fit for me, and I fitted right in. Safe in the clamour of the fire, like a god. Or a demon. Alive. Not smiling, nor weeping. I just lay there, just lay there. The flames raged round me, freeing me of old memories, drenching me in new visions, and then, inevitably, the distinction between memory and vision melted away and my entry into a new life became effortless, ordinary; the new life itself became normal. The thing about bombs, you see, is that they burrow deep inside to do their work, so on the surface everything looks ordinary, normal.

What a scene. The cafe in flames from my explosion. Martyred, bloody, people fleeing. Some escaped. Others dehydrated into smoke. Smoke and cinders. Waiters, children, chairs, plates.

And him.

Eighteen years old. His remains returned home nailed into a sarkari box. He had spread out over the length and breadth of the cafe. Collected and sealed in an official box, he returned home. Like all those others did, caught snatching a quick samosa before the exam, both turning to ashes before they could eat or be eaten.

Scraps. Every year, reports in newspapers. Ashes dripping darkly from the news. And my testimony. My first-person accounts. An eyewitness. Lying quietly right in the middle of the fire, a god, a demon, an empty space. Safe and sound in the midst of swirling lumps of flesh.

It was only when the cafe had burnt to the ground and the police burst in, sirens screaming, that they came upon that inert mass in the shape of a three-year-old child, red, crawling with ants, silent and still, but alive. And the ants eating it, or protecting it.

2

Times are such, people say. Ma is silent. Times are such, they say, that children leave home only to return in bits and pieces inside sarkari boxes. They leave home in search of their roots: *who are you, your ancestors, who am I?* Then they return in shreds. Such are the times, they say. Ma is silent.

But he had questions, that body in pieces, whose death I live day in and day out. 'Who am I,' he asked, clear and sharp, and the replies pour in still from newspapers, research articles, pamphlets, broadcasts, from me . . . 'I will go to where you come from,' he had said to his father, who was his father first and later, mine. Or never mine, maybe, because forever after, at meeting after meeting he would mutter, looking vacant, but sort of at me, that 'in fact someone else' should have been there, someone else should have blown up, which people understood as meaning him, the father of the son, but I suspected it meant me. I should have been there, in the spot that tore his son to bits. Not in the empty space ringed by fire.

That space into which Ma descended in order to become my mother, before which she was only his, and returned then with both of us in her lap, me and the pieces in the box, and forever after tried to stop herself from slipping through the cracks, grabbing hold of me on the way like *I'm* the one who's gone, pulling at me like she's pulling at him, pulling him back.

But he's not me. I'm not him. But then, I'm not me, either.

So? Isn't this how everyone lives? We lead a life which is not ours and a life leads us, to which we don't belong. One that will not own us, one that we will not own. There we go, slipping away between our own fingers!

Such a beautiful boy, people would murmur, remembering him. This one is sweet too, patting me kindly. Always thus, always—first the departed son; only then, the son present.

But maybe I've just become too cynical. For that son was not unbeautiful, as you can see from the countless photographs amidst which I live. They show too, what he could have become had he not been torn to shreds. Philosopher, surrounded by books. Rock star guitarist. Champion swimmer vanquishing the ocean. Arms around parents, the support of their old age. Sometimes just their son, spoilt and loving, popping a snack into his mouth, as he would have in the cafe before he was blown up. And by my bed, three years old, wearing just a T-shirt, all naked below, one hand holding the red rose of the nation's leader, the other hand resting on the new television set, both in their infancy. Ironically, seeing *that* photograph people would always ask if it was me, otherwise everything was always him, while I was neither him nor me!

Fair, light-eyed, father would say, which *I* wasn't. *Vilayati*, folk at his village had marvelled, stroking his golden brown hair. Crimson with beauty his cheeks, mine aflame with embarrassment, no resemblance at all.

Slaves of the West, I sneer inwardly at my father's pride. Free citizens, educated, aware! And proud of fair skin and light eyes!

My father, the lone educated person in his village, a 'big man' there, undoubtedly. There, in his native village to which he had gone back on a visit, and with him his son—before he was blown to smithereens.

3

Like kings visiting their subjects.

The car stopped where the narrow road wound far ahead to the border, and the bushes on either side practically disappeared behind the crowd of villagers waiting to greet them with folded hands. The village nestled, invisible behind mud dunes. The two of them strode in proudly, kicking up the dust, and from the dry earth emerged more men, more children, and then women too, and soon the huts were visible, and the two sole concrete structures in which they would stay, and on a thin wire swayed a light bulb in the breeze, like a piece of cloth fluttering on a line to dry, but with an air of being the lord of all it surveyed. Like that father and like his son, revelling in their royal status. The son so thrilled that even three days of constipation could not dim his excitement—a constipation that ended only when a newspaper was spread out, a broken chair on it, and he sat in the chair, producing pieces that the newspaper collected.

See how some random event can come to foretell a whole life! Because thereafter, throughout another lifetime—mine—newspapers kept collecting pieces—pieces of my life.

Life insists that coincidences be sought. That signs be found, that they be matched to one another. That a narrative be shaped.

So that's how it was. He (and I too?) still intact, not in pieces but joined together; happy memories of that village, of that region from where the father was, and therefore he too (and I . . .?).

He came back home then, with *his* father, with the beginning of that dream in *his* heart which would seek *its* completion, *its* remainder, *its* end.

4

He had this irrepressible curiosity, Father said of him, 'Where am I from, whose am I?'

'You belong to the stars,' Ma had said, 'and to me.'

'So fetch me a ladder,' he said as a child, 'to reach me to the skies. And I'll find myself.'

Once again that echo from the future. Reflections, in conversations past, of conversations to come.

'And that's why when he grew up,' he said, 'Let me go *there* to study. You're from there, Father, what's it like, that place, its soil? Where our village is? That famous university nearby, I'll study there, let me go.'

'To be scared all the time? Scared everywhere? I won't live like that. I want it. I *will* go.'

'But there?' Ma nagged, anxiety on Father's brow. 'And with such a name, no one can even tell where you're from and who you are.'

'It's all right,' Father consoled her, and himself. 'My village is not far, our relatives are there . . .'

'And what about the riots?' Ma snapped.

'That's just politics.'

'And this subject he wants to study not taught anywhere else? At least let's wait till the elections, let's see who forms the new government,' Ma insisted stubbornly.

'Be quiet,' said Father, cajoling his own concern to silence, shutting up Ma. 'That university is famous the world over. And what will a new government change?'

At that he spoke, in whose place I remain, 'Look at the two of you, carrying on as if it's not college I'm about to enter, but the doors of death!'

He wouldn't let up. 'Then you may as well say, never step out. Not today, not ever, not anywhere. Remember that man who bent down to pick up a packet of milk and down came the awning on him, like a guillotine? And the other chap who went out of his gate just to take a leak, imagine, not even to shit, touched a bare wire and was electrocuted? Just like that. Never any electricity when you need it, but of course, at that moment, flowing in full force through the wire?'

And thus the future revealed itself—but only when it had passed—little by little, in these words.

Ma roped everyone into her campaign, instantly enlisted everybody—to din some sense into him, stop him somehow, not allow him to go. Become a policeman who knows the blackest secrets of the government, become an underworld don who knows the pulse of criminals, become a doctor, teacher, lawyer, mother, father, friend, foe, be whatever it takes to prevail upon him. Laugh, sing, joke, plead, do whatever you can, pledge your heart, your life, in any way, somehow, just convince him, stop him.

'Go.' Ma said in the end. 'You never ask for anything. How can I refuse? Go, my son.'

'You're the world's best mom,' they all say he said, their eyes wet that she let him go.

He went, a rule book round his neck. He was not to venture into the sensitive areas of the town, nor into the desolate ones, nor the crowded ones, no visiting fairs, no getting on to buses, no loafing about in the dark, nor where ruffians lurk, such as railway stations, bus depots.

Stick to safe areas.

In and around the university. Where nothing has ever happened.

Like that cafe. Safe, the university cafe. Where nothing has ever happened.

5

Fragments. Ashes.

Ceiling fans caught in the molten fluid poses of a danseuse. Crockery, bottles, napkins, laid out in rows, pitch-black, exhibits of art. The cafe itself, the black-themed dream of an artist. Abstract art. Bits and pieces that could be chairs, or tables, or idlis, sambar, gulab jamun, pav-bhaji. Bits and pieces that could be people, could be boys and girls poised to enter the university. Broken bits which, joined up, would be nineteen people if the breaker knew how to join them. If he had been Brahma, Vishnu and Mahesh, all rolled into one.

Nineteen people. Yet to be identified. Bits and pieces, unclaimed still.

To identify—to separate from the mass. But here, to identify meant to try and put together that which had been separated so violently.

And there I was, whole and unharmed, nestling in the lap of the ants or being lapped up by them. Bits and pieces of nineteen people and one three-year-old bit, which could have been part of anything, perhaps of the bomb, or was it the bomb itself, or a devil or a god, who appears at night even now, scratch scratch, bringing the ants to scrape away my armour of sleep scratch scratch, so that once again I'm that three-year-old in the empty space and once again the roar of flames leaping close and once again the pieces of the eighteen-year-old filling the darkness and everything falling away, falling away, a heart pounding away, the explosion always about to happen, and the cover of sleep scraped away scratch scratch and the night stretching long and interminable and somehow, somehow it must be passed . . .

My entire body breaks out into red rashes.

6

Nineteen bodies, once flesh and blood. Now sprayed all over.

And another. An empty space.

The process of identification begins. A shirt collar. A half-burnt ten-rupee note. An admission form, transformed into the intriguing map of some unknown country. A reference letter, its script yellow and brown, like a parchment from a museum. Scorched heaps. How to identify, and what?

The police fanned out all over the town. Anyone missing could be in those ashes. *No no*, their families were horrified, couldn't be him, that's just his way, he would often stay away from home for days . . .

The cops were unconvinced. One two three—they went on identifying. Gradually, sixteen heaps were formally identified. Name, father's name, father's father's name. Seventeen, eighteen, nineteen were left. Two were then re-imagined out of the cinders and recreated into bodies. The nineteenth remained. Him.

And one more. Me. He. Me. Who?

His picture in the papers. My picture too, in the papers. No phone calls for me. For him, a mother, a father, a phone call.

'Not him,' Father said firmly. 'It's impossible. He went there just five days ago. He was so eager to go there. That's all. That is all.'

Phone calls upon phone calls, no other work gets done. Father at the phone, Ma sitting beside him. Father dialling, Ma's eyes shut tight; Father dialling, Ma staring wildly. Call the university, call the police, call the newspapers. Call religious bodies, call interfaith bodies. Call the big and the powerful. Call this person's contacts, call that person's contacts.

What did you find out, what? Only that there was a blast. In the university cafe. For the first time. They haven't yet identified the survivors, the injured, the dead.

'Don't worry,' neighbours and acquaintances said to them, in that moment when the ground spun beneath their feet, breaking all speed limits.

'Don't worry,' Father said to Ma, echoing the others. 'He called just yesterday, didn't he, saying he was planning a trip to the neighbouring town, to see one of the wonders of the world? He must have gone there, that's all . . . That is all.'

The identification continued. Into that overpopulated city that fateful day had poured hundreds from outside. Entrance forms, exams, young children, their dreams glowing on their parents' faces, an ocean of people. Anything could have happened, a bomb could have exploded, it did, people could have died, they did, but some could have survived . . .

'The list of the injured still isn't complete,' Father snapped at Ma. 'Don't keep disturbing them with phone calls.' As if Ma was the one making the calls!

When the phone was in *his* hands, a seal on Ma's lips.

Let the identification continue. Of hearts, fingers, pakodas, livers, kidneys . . .

The list is awaited with the eagerness reserved for the university admission list. One more name appears. Is it my child?

Where has he got admission? Among the survivors, the remaining, the departed? On which list?

One name, then another and another. Only his didn't appear anywhere.

Mere coincidence? This one alone remained unidentified, and that one. His remains and I remain! In our respective shapes. Both unclaimed, unknown. He and I. Did somewhere our differences get enmeshed, to remain entangled for evermore? He and me. He or me? One dead, yet to be identified. One survivor, yet to be identified. Which one died, which one survived? No really, I'm serious, do we really know?

It's all a mess. One is in pieces; the other, an abandoned piece. Me, smoked and suffocated. He, smoked and smashed up. He dead, me alive, both nameless. And who knows, maybe he was alive and I was dead and both were missing?

Waiting for our names to be posted in the list. Waiting for our pictures in the newspapers to be recognized, for someone to bring him back, for someone to take me away.

But. No phone call, nobody, no wonder-of-the-world. Just that Father is summoned to sign a paper.

Father's signature is required. No need for Ma.

7

But there's always need for Ma. Father collects the ashes in his palms, Mother recognizes the pieces. Ma knows which button she had sewn on to which shirt. *She* knows, not Father. And she knows exactly how low the drawstring on his pyjama had hung, that she had wound round a pencil to tuck into its waistband. And this is the pocket into which she had slipped the good luck toffee; if only he had popped it into his mouth, wouldn't her motherly blessings have evaporated the bomb before it could explode?

It was the mothers, not the police, who finally completed the job. They landed up, all the mothers who had sent off their children for higher studies so that they could take on the world. They landed up—to tell apart idli from heart, gulab jamun from intestine from kidney from liver. What was that in the ashes, a bit of idli fluffed in steam, or the guts of her child, warmed and stirred with her lifeblood?

They came in buses and cars, the mothers, past burnt-out factories, burnt-out shops, past blackened skeletons of buses, past every revealing sign; all the way up to the cafe.

The cafe was burnt down completely when the women arrived, their tears and sobs frozen. Sky azure, the sun bright. The mothers like beams of brilliance descending not from buses, but from somewhere higher up.

Life is an epic, and every expression is a sign, every atom a significant portent.

The cafe was now suddenly in a 'sensitive area'. Rioters amok in the city. The cafe a magnet for danger.

Like a band of disciplined terrorists the women surrounded the cafe. The police on guard stepped back in awe. As the women set foot in the cafe, the sky darkened. Clouds gathered and thunder rolled. Thunder and torrential rain.

Every single thing a sign, every atom adding up to a tale. No one came any longer to the cafe. Even ghosts crave ambiguous flickers of shade and light. But nothing ambiguous about the clear black soot of the cafe. Only soot—the scent, soot; vision, soot; silence, soot. The floor, soot. The air, soot. The roof, soot. The past, soot. The button she had sewed on. The pyjama string she had wound in.

The mothers' feet floated, by a hairsbreadth of mother-love above the burnt floor. Their scorched glances swept the cafe.

Their feet would not descend. Who knew where . . . on whom . . .? Gently they began to glide. And as they opened the doors of the burnt metal cupboards, shadows of smoke and ash floated out and curled around them. Soot rose from the depths of the floor, its tendrils curling up, kissing their floating feet. In the devastated cafe, ash swirled around the floating mothers, flickering soft as candles, searching, here is my child . . . here . . . and here.

And this is how Ma was floating when by a hairsbreadth of mother-love under her feet she sensed a bit of space in which a three-year-old could just fit.

No ash flew up from there, and gently, Ma lowered her feet.

8

Ma recognized her son, God knows how. Where her finger pointed, there lay his remains. These were sorted out respectfully, collected and sealed with full official glory into a box and handed over to Ma by the most senior police official in town, so that she might clasp her child to her bosom and take him home.

Announcements on the radio. The last bit has been identified. Her eighteen-year-old son a household name. Pictures in newspapers. Of the box, passing from one hand to the other. Into Ma's hands. Of Ma reaching out a hand to gather up one son, and raising her gaze to make another her own.

That's exactly how the picture looks today. Ma has just said, that's my child, and is about to say, I want that other child. The picture is the hinge between those two moments. The camera shutter clicks, and immediately afterwards she says what she is about to, in the picture.

She has said it. In that moment of her bereavement, her words cannot go unheard. Nor the orders of the police official. Subordinates click their boots and spring into obedient action.

The police van sweeps up Ma and dashes through the streets. Ma alights at the police station. Gun-toting men lead her inside. A policewoman is changing my soiled nappy.

Ma stands at the door.

I was staring blankly. The way I did. The sound of the bomb and the smell of the smoke filling me inside and eyes unseeingly open. Khaki on parade to the right and left of me, the stomp of boots like cannons echoing in my eardrums. The touch of indifferent hands from which arose unwanted, unfamiliar smells that meant nothing to me. My eyes locked shut, and my mouth too, the focus of efforts by the entire police force to push in a few drops of milk.

Then came the smell. I knew it, the smell of soot. I opened my eyes. Ma stepped into the room. My glance locked on the sarkari box in her hands. My lower lip pouted in a silent sob. I was not crying yet. Ma picked me up. Father went off to add one more signature to one more official paper.

One more file closed, the police must be relieved. No one had laid claim to the three-year-old in the papers but Ma.

Nobody recognized that three-year-old.

Not even I did. Not even after all these years added to the three.

I cannot recognize, I cannot own, that three-year-old imprisoned in the photograph tucked away in Ma's locker, nor recognize that second—the first!—son in the ashes locked into the official box and sitting in the locker too.

We had set out together, the box and I, to this house. He, incomplete in his return; I, incomplete in my beginning.

9

How much does an official box measure? Difficult to say. The size of anything official is deceptive. As for this one, this box containing the son, it's unique, what can its size possibly be? Big enough to hold a fistful of ash? Or as big as he should have been by rights at his death, laid out in full? Who can tell measurements and such when all there is to measure with, are inch tapes and weighing scales? When size changes with the advancing and retarding of age—the bigger I become, the smaller he gets, and so does the box containing him.

Sometimes, alone in my room—which was his, and is, and will remain—I imagine getting up and then bending double to enter that box or chest or drawer or casket or container or urn or carton labelled 'freight'. Flattened against its cold floor I wait in queue with the other luggage at the airport, to go under the X-ray and flash my guts on the screen.

The government paid for their air tickets, Father's and Ma's, to bring him and me back home. The reward for releasing them from two files. I, secure in Ma's lap, coming to be her son, he, hopping and skipping along as freight on the conveyer belt.

How does it feel to be freight? To bounce along the conveyor belt? Does it hurt? Or is it fun? Cold and dark inside, invisible voices from outside? The screech of trolleys, the squeak of wheels, shouts, *be quick we're late*, in this language and that, *last call, flight closed*, panic, all the hubbub of the airport from inside the box. All clear, green signal, off I go on the conveyor belt, bon voyage!

Does the ash give a small excited jump inside the box? Just a little one?

Or is the box jostled by the conveyer belt caught at a curve? Locked inside. Stuck and shuddering in place, I feel only the belt jerking under me. Someone notices and gives me a push. Back on the rails I go chugging along.

Does that person know what it was he just pushed?

The airport official has no idea either. 'What's inside that?'

he barks, suspiciously eying Father.

Anybody could be a terrorist, any luggage could contain RDX.

Father fumbles for the official letter.

'My son,' hisses Ma.

The official has not heard, or not understood. 'X-ray!' barks the voice box fitted at his throat.

There is confusion. The official stares at the letter Father hands him like he doesn't know how to read. Images flash on the monitor. Other officials rush up: let it go, it's . . . *that*. Suddenly everyone stands up respectfully.

Reporters, bystanders, security staff, gawking travellers, cleaning staff, all gather—*oh it's that story, it's that story, oh for a camera.*

It is all there in the picture, the swing of the hair, the flow of the conversation, the V for Victory flashed by a smart alec, the briskness of the airport employees, the flashy new interiors of the new airport. But not that, the silence, the shiver of which ran down every spine as the box went through the X-ray scanner. What had shown up on the monitor? An object or a human? Flowers or a bomb? Pebbles or seashells? When clothes and skin were stripped off by the X-ray, what showed up?

I lie in my—his—room, imagining being the ashy remains glowing on the monitor and I smile. My child's eyes remember a box like a coffin; the adult I am now, sees a little ceremonial urn in Ma's locker. In it you'll find, desolate in the smoky ash, traces of ivory glinting like eyes.

10

Sensational as it was for the town that the parents returned with their son in a box, it was no less sensational that they brought back another in their arms. The highly regarded father, the fame of the sons, the story of the terrible tragedy, the lively, loveable mother. That one child should depart like that, another arrive like this—they couldn't stop talking about it.

There are cameras. Photographers, journalists, bureaucrats, politicians. Those alighting with the box are confused. They need to be told what to do, how to be. Now and forever after.

There was a general demand for an interfaith gathering, a sarvadharmasabha. Arrangements were made. A large, old building, filled with history and with the echoes of old religions. On the walls, portraits of leaders, while below, portrait-like, competing religious leaders sat in brotherly rows. The hall was buzzing with crowds. And amidst the hubbub sat the box, silent.

When a public bomb fragments your son, the fragments of your son become public property. Their son is the box presiding over the assembly. On the stage, before a picture of himself.

In the picture, he's a schoolboy making a speech. In the box, he's in fragments. Like chief guests, we were seated right in front of him. I, hiding inside my red rash, Ma's stunned gaze sometimes on the picture, sometimes sliding to the box; Father sort of smiling when he caught someone's eye and sort of crying when the box caught his. Not quite certain which expression to settle on.

The priest, the maulvi, the pundit, the saint, the ascetic, the tunic, the turban, the beads, the mantra, the sermon, the bhajan, the song, the melody—raising this world up to the next. How beautiful the passage from this world. How beautiful, grief; how quiet, serene, pure, glowing softly in the light of the lamps and the candles. Like the iridescence from a fine glass chandelier, it drifts gently over the hall.

The school principal fights back sobs recounting the happy moments spent with the boy in the box. He imitates the boy imitating him, at which he had scolded him, but turning away, had hidden a smile. He was so naughty but so promising too . . . there was so much he had to accomplish.

Relatives reduce everyone to tears with their memories, friends sing the songs they had sung together, leaders who had never met him wax eloquent: he belonged to all of us, the star of his generation, the symbol of those grand possibilities that the barbaric, immoral, inhuman forces want to grind into the dust, but we will not permit it, we will not let him die, he is not dead, he lives on in all of us, he keeps urging us not to let these evil forces win, we bow to the brave parents who bore him.

Please say something . . . someone bends over Ma. She doesn't hear.

You please . . . they request Father and lead him to the stage. He looks lost, his lips tremble.

He says something. Something about the child who gave them eighteen wonderful years and all the love and respect in the world. *I am so lucky that I came into the world to be his father.*

At that moment it was decided that for the rest of his life this is what he would say, at meetings year after year, in interviews, among friends, at gatherings, at street corners, when alone, and often when he behaved as if he was alone, as if he couldn't see me nearby, within earshot.

People keep filing up to the stage. Some offer flowers, others, garlands. Touch the box gently. Some with their foreheads. The box sinks deeper and deeper into the flowers and garlands. Sinks till only a corner shows above the flowers. Sinks until it drowns in a flowery grave.

A sound escapes Ma's throat that belongs to no human tongue. She doesn't drop me, holds me tight, so tight that my rashes throb with pain, she rips past the line of people and up the stage. Holding me still, she sinks to her knees and bending over her son, she begins to tear the flowers off him. The stage is a sea of blossoms, I cling like a baby monkey to Ma, and finally she has dredged up the box from the depths of the flowers.

Then she opens her arms and spreads them over the box, presses her face against it. Both her sons in her embrace. Ma's palms cover the earth. *Enough, I want nothing more, enough* . . .

11

Finally it's all over.

It's only when it's all over that you begin to feel it. Like the moment Father turned the key and opened the door.

Or let's say you don't feel it at the moment the bomb explodes. But afterwards, all your life it keeps exploding, again and again; and each time you know it has exploded, all over again.

Or you could say that a bomb is something you can never free yourself from. Because after it has exploded, it leaves the tumult outside and sneaks inside you quietly, crouches there, hidden and ballooning. Rolls out at will like a ball bouncing out at a chance nudge, but with the same familiar terrifying explosion.

No sooner had Father entered the house, cradling the box, than the bomb erupted. Suddenly everything in the house was swooping through the air. Flames leaping.

That sofa with the broken springs, that hollow where he had jumped up and down defiantly as a child. Once again the child leaped . . .

That dining table where he had drunk cup after cup of tea and Father would nag, *so much tea; in my time, boys drank milk.* Once again the tea splashed . . .

Those stairs that went up to his room, where the light would be on, and Father would go on and on about how in his time nights were for sleeping and days for studying. The lights went on, and the shout came down: *Mom, coffee . . .!*

The son comes sliding down the banisters. *No no*! Father had bellowed in another age. All around rose the remains of despair. Father held on carefully to the ashes.

Ma did not see the explosion. She wiped her sandals on the doormat. Dust flew up. Touched the arm of the chair. Dust on her finger. Touched the table. There too, dust. Went into the kitchen and opened the fridge. Cold smoke enveloped her face. Quickly, she pulled out milk, dal, meat, sniffed at them, flung them in the trash. Then she took down the bunch of keys off a peg and began opening rooms, cupboards. Dusting things with the loose end of her sari. In the bathroom, she threw the stored water into the flush, scrubbed the bucket clean and put it under the tap to fill. Put water on to boil on the stove. Busy, busy. Opening windows and cleaning the panes, pulling down curtains to shake them free of dust. A foot here, a hand there. Everything in pieces.

Will not see. Will not hear. Just keeps sinking into her own eyes. The fish-shaped shadows surrounding them turning darker and darker. Her pupils lay dead, swallowed into the belly of the fish. They can't see and they can't hear.

That's why she missed noticing that each time she opened a window or a door, yet another shred flew out from the explosion inside Father. Love, desire, hope, humour, keenness, softness, curiosity, simplicity, the eight essences, the ninth rasa, peace, all the emotions that go into the making of a man, blasted into the galaxy, never to be found, never to be whole again, suspended somewhere in the cosmos.

It had happened again. The bomb had exploded. Everything in ashes. The house in ashes. The son safe inside the sarkari box.

And there was that one space, empty, the size of a three-year-old. Once again I was flung free—safe, whole, untouched by the incident, saved, or abandoned, just coated in soot, expressionless under the red rash.

12

I grow, and the story grows.

Usually people want to be told a story in such a way that they don't feel it's only a story. They want pitch-dark film theatres and 3D celluloid screens with characters so real that we can step outside our lives and lead theirs. But it's just a momentary illusion, the fun of living the joys and sorrows of others, momentary release from the creature that grates, grates, under our skin. The magic of being someone else for a while.

And the enormous relief. Oh the relief that the tears spilling from our eyes do not mourn our own fate, that our grief is but passing, it's but a dream, a video, a film, a book. The story is over, our lives are steady again. On screen or on the page will flash 'The End,' the lights will come on, everything around us will be familiar again, secure again. This body will become ours, will become whole. Not in pieces like Father's or Ma's or the son's.

Well, that's up to you, and up to them. I refuse to get into a quarrel about all of this. Aren't there enough quarrels all around already? After all, it's thanks to just such a quarrel that this story, or whatever it is, exists. Surely not every storyteller has to be like God, omnipresent, omniscient, the Creator? Let a simple act be what it is. When an actress gyrates on screen seemingly naked, but in a skin-coloured suit so that she can say I wasn't naked, whom is she fooling? If the viewer thinks she's naked, how does it help her to know she was not?

When one's life is someone else's, can anyone tell whose life it really is? Where is the one, where is the other? If not one's own, whose life is it? The story I tell, is it about this life which is on right now—mine? Or is it about that life which is over, but is still going on—his?

Because how does one understand that life which may not really be one's life? If one experiences the act of love in all its intensity and it turns out to have been a lie, was it ever really love? What was it? Do I exist? Or not?

Usually people want a story to be simple, to reveal itself on its own, predictably. But different times insist on different things. The times I live in insist that ambiguity should hide behind each clarity, or perhaps this is the way it really is. A suffocating grey ambiguity.

I chase the story, the story chases me, time chases its characters, they chase time, and behind it all is the bomb, and also ahead.

13

So the house is his or mine, and it's me and my life or he and his. I don't enjoy confusing things, but how else do I put it? Even if I could choose, what would I choose—my three years or his eighteen? Somewhere amongst it all beats my pulse and my parents' and not his of course, but the throb of each pulse is his, really. And no one knows for sure about the day the bomb exploded and the two of us were scattered, I whole and he in pieces, whether that day was my birthday or his deathday.

If you have any doubts, go check out the papers and magazines. Not one of them ignored the day. It was celebrated like a festival. A day of stark grief. The day of his coronation. A death so sparklingly alive that many a life pales in comparison.

A death that became his birth. And mine.

Nobody said it quite that way though, that his deathday was my birthday. How could they—his deathday my birthday! Although really, that was the only known day of my birth. Instead, they chose another date as my birthday, a date on which even the idea of me had not been born, either in this house, or anywhere in the world. The date on which

Father had sat out on the verandah, listening to Ma's groans as the midwife and the surgeon stood vigil, and he was born. Me too.

I mean I got his birthday, like I got his Ma, his Father, his pen, his cup, his music, those clothes of his that fit me, his spectacle frame redone with my shades for the sun, his room, his this, his that. For Ma parted with nothing of his, didn't put away his stuff in any store room, nor donated it in charity to any temple, mosque or synagogue. Ma was not for charity.

Unless of course, you see me as charity.

So I would be all spruced up on his birthday, arranged in front of his favourite cinnamon and cardamom cake in the shape of his unfinished dream, a guitar, all iced with gooey chocolate. *Blow*, they said, and I would not.

Always a single candle, perhaps to bridge the gap of confused calculations about when I turned four, he would have turned nineteen and when I turned five, he would complete twenty. And they said *blow* and I would not.

Did I understand then? When did I understand, when did I become capable of understanding, that as I grew in years, it was *his* age that was being calculated in the eyes of the guests? And on everyone's part, the insistence that we will remember with joy the one who gave us joy, not by shrouding him in sadness, which would be a victory for the murderers. He would have wanted everyone to be happy.

And his will be done.

He was everywhere, smiling down from his blown-up pictures on the walls. Growing each year a little. There would be just one candle on the cake but people knew how to count the invisible ones. And from the first time they said *blow* I refused.

Puff out your cheeks so, they would coax me, trying to teach me how. His friends would become monkeys, bears, puffing away, making fools of themselves.

Blow my child, whispered Ma right into my ear, but even then it felt like she was not speaking to me, and not speaking with her mouth, but her words were coming from those distant eyes and were getting entangled somewhere far inside her dead-fish pupils.

He doesn't know how to blow, Father said. Not in the way one says such things to children to make them do the opposite, but in the way he would say *he can't speak even at this age when* . . . He wouldn't complete his sentence, but said it all in the way he looked at me like I was an empty cast in which someone else should have been, alas.

14

Someone overlooked by even fire and gunpowder, learns naturally to lie forgotten. And learns to forget. The knowledge of breathing, speaking, chewing, all locked away deep inside, face expressionless, leaving Father wringing his hands and forcing him to be the one to speak.

This boy will never speak, he said and turned his eyes away to space, seeking some lost piece of himself.

This was on the birthday. His friends making a noise. Laughing pictures. Fragrance in the air.

Ma tried to put the first slice of cake into my mouth. His friends clapped and began to sing. *Happy birthday to you!*

My tongue stayed glued to my palate. Ma tried to push in bits with a spoon, into a narrow cave cutting away with an axe. The cake got pushed in.

So then the cake was stuck to my palate.

I did not swallow it. *I will not swallow it*. I lay inside my skin, expressionless.

His friends had done up the dining room, telling his stories afresh. They had tied a bunch of balloons in a knot above the table. A riot of colours waved in my face. Yellow, red, blue, green. And purple.

Slowly I saw them turning black.

Pepsi, Limca and beer did the rounds. Father was trying to knit back into himself one of his bits floating in space, taking out a picture from an album, recounting its story over sips of beer.

In the picture Ma was sitting in the rocking chair kept in the room above, with the broken son whole in her lap. No longer a child, all grown up. Taller than his mother. Raising his hand in a toast, holding up a mug of foaming beer. Both laughing, mother and son. Father was jabbering away, as he did at any odd moment, whenever a lost part of himself floated down from space. It was his first beer, Father said. See how the rascal sits in his Ma's lap to drink it! It was his eighteenth birthday and he declared, now I'm an adult and I will drink!

No one said it was his last birthday. Because in a way what was being celebrated now was also his birthday, even if mine too. Celebrating and saying *it was his first beer*. Not his last beer too, no one says that. Which he gulped down sitting in his mother's lap.

No one says it was the last time he sat in her lap. Then off he went seeking admission in one place and gained it in completely another. *Jana tha Japan pahunch gaye Cheen!*

Ma looked like she had gone with him and died with him.

I stare silently at the balloons going black. Slowly, the balloon lurking in my dark recesses begins to roll out. About to explode. Scattering everything. Ma, Father, me, friends, the party, pictures. All sewed with a single thread, all threaded into one anticipation. Of the explosion. Of the balloon.

After all, what is a bomb? A needle that threads together scattered pieces. A cannon ball that falls from the sky. A sack that tears open and scatters. A love story that breaks and binds. A 'him' and a 'me' . . . A life which . . . which . . . and then . . . then . . .

Then someone had picked up a fork and was boisterously bursting the balloons one by one. Burst . . . exploded . . . I began to sob, to sob uncontrollably.

Everyone was struck dumb. *Why, what's wrong with him? Oh dear, did you want a balloon then?* Leaping up, they began pulling at the balloons and handing them to me.

15

As it is, he and I are all mixed up, and to add to the confusion, I go to the same school he used to go. The teacher hands me over to Ma like a balloon on a string every day, with a new bit of advice each time. Teach him this, teach him that. Sometimes it's reading, sometimes writing, sometimes colouring. But also how to speak, how to sit, how to eat. The problem is, the teacher tells Ma, he knows, but will not do anything.

Ma's retort, why am I sending him to school if I have to teach him at home?

Home and school all mixed up, teacher and Ma mixed up. And he and I are mixed up anyway.

But the school could not throw me out. They allowed me to be there. The other one had learnt so much here, this one too must be taught something, somehow.

Whisper whisper . . . *this one is that one, he's the one* . . . all over school. While I shrink away from everyone, waiting for Ma to come.

I would grab her hand and rush out. Pulling her along. Out of the school and into the narrow alleys squeezed between congested buildings, pushing through in haste as if they were about to become narrower. Not a sliver of space between the houses for breeze, sky, hills, fire, not a crevice for a thought to pass, my breath weighs heavy here. These heavy breaths filling the air around me, are they his, or mine?

Careful, Ma reprimands me.

Faster, faster, my tongue stutters.

As if somewhere on the roofs of those gray crammed houses, someone sits in wait, waiting to slap down my choking breath as it rises.

Are you feeling hot? Ma asks.

I keep running as if the next moment and, the moment after that, are all closing in on me threateningly. *Zero in on him. Zero in and then . . .*

By the time we get home my body is covered in the same red rash and Ma says anxiously, how this child feels the heat.

The moment we enter the house I want to tear free and run. So that I don't show it, I hold my breath and climb up the stairs slowly, slowly. Inside, my body is hurtling at top speed, but outside, it's creeping slowly up the stairs. Counting my steps helps to keep a steady pace. One . . . two . . . three . . . ten . . . turn right at the potted plant he had brought . . . past it, once again one . . . two . . . three . . . four . . . handle. Door. Room.

Darkness. Closed window. No sky outside. Just dust and bricks and cement burying you alive.

You can see me there at the window. See me growing up. Ma sees me grow up when she massages oil on my body before bathing me, soothing my rashes. She massages gently, careful about both her sons.

Her hands run lovingly over my body as they did over his. She keeps murmuring as she massages me. Tiny hands just

like these. Tiny feet just like these. Crisp cucumbers—I could *bite* them. Cheeks like rasgullas. Sweet-sweet. Here my sugar pastry, mmm . . . yummy yum. And jalebi . . . where's my jalebi . . . where . . . lets look for it . . . here? Here? Giggle now, come on, tickle tickle.

She tickles her son. And a laugh churns up out of me. The one in the photograph sees it all, hears it all. He sees Ma massage oil into my skin and hears her coo—my baby will grow big, with fingers so long, legs so strong, he will become great and famous.

She keeps talking as she massages me after school to grow me up: Ma's here, my child, you're safe. Ma will teach you everything. Writing, reading, singing, jumping. Never be scared. Ma will protect you. From scolding teachers, mean children, speeding cars, scary insects, you're safe in my tummy. If a nasty man comes along, my stare will frighten him away—gobble me up but don't you dare touch my baby. No one dares harm you, my child, for you have your Ma.

She would massage me—Ma, filling me with him through the pores of her fingertips, filling me with him, and saving him and saving him.

16

It doesn't necessarily happen that a new son is able to scatter happiness simply by replacing the old. On the contrary, it could just be that the old has returned as the new, in order to bring joy again. After all, the new one just lies in his empty space, just lies there, who notices? It's the old one who is buried again and again and then resurrected each time.

When the doorbell rings, for a fraction of a second, Ma's hands stop in the midst of her work. But then she disappears again behind her dead-fish eyes and goes back to what she was doing.

On the outside, she goes about her work efficiently. As if all of us, the home, the world, flowerpots, bouquets, are machine parts to be oiled properly, the bearings well worked, the screws tightened. It's not Ma's style to be careless with the machine.

But with herself, she couldn't care less. Smoking as if to vanish into the smoke. This is how she has taken to smoking cigarettes, losing herself in the rings of smoke.

Father opens the door and in comes a bunch of people from his community. Father was born into a community, so what if he had consciously broken away from it, in his marriage and his life, flouting all its rules of religion and caste. They are here, his people, to reassure him and to resurrect his son.

And after all, what they said made sense: 'When a son is lost, the loss is not just one person's. It is an entire conspiracy to spread terror, to destroy all our promising children, our next generation. We can't force you to come to this meeting if you don't wish to, but the meeting will be held. He would have done us proud. We can't let his death go to waste, his life is a flaming torch.'

After all, everyone in a community can't be bad. They weren't saying anything wrong. They have a point. The community has a human side too, not just an oppressive one.

'We too want a beautiful, better world,' they said. 'Like our dear child did.'

They glanced once at Ma and then looked away. Because it's the fathers who make up the community. Or was it because they feared losing themselves in the hollows of those eyes?

They look over at the stairs, from behind which I peek out.

'Bring him too,' they said, and I hid myself a bit more. 'Our child has given him life. He has a new beginning, an inspiration, a home, a path.'

'That boy will never speak,' came Father's voice.

I sneaked a look at him, and he was wandering in space again where his pieces were strewn, which, if he could gather together, would make him one whole person.

Ha! Which is the boy who will never speak? Smugly, I stuck my tongue to my palate and looked around. From every wall, his photographs looked down on me. His things, his favourite colours, his tastes, everywhere. The boy who will never speak again!

I started to inch away, back slumped against the railing, my eyes on the wall ahead. His photographs passing before my eyes like scenes from a speeding train. Like he's moving and I'm still. Padded up for cricket, he plants one firm foot in front of him. I shrink back. Bat poised, he swings it, and *there*, slashing the air. I flinch. A spring in his waist, he veers around, touches the ball and sends it soaring.

I keep moving back one step at a time. He is the one frozen in place, I am the one lending him speed and movement. Back, and further back, till I reach the door to the room in which I sit listlessly, tongue glued to the roof of my mouth. I get up only to steal a glance below where the guests are, or to see what's happening up there, with the one I brought to life, what is he doing in his picture. A last glimpse of my friend. I look fondly at the sporty cap he wears.

This is not the cap which, after his departure, the people of the community clapped on his head with the aid of digital technology.

17

Of course any father would do this.

This is the line I gave the girl who is soon to enter this story or whatever it is. Of course any father would have done it.

Not only now in this era of the global magic of the bomb—one sneeze, and poof, everything up in the air. But even before, when people disappeared, their loved ones would wait and wait for them. Wouldn't they? They needed a living corpse.

Yes, living. To touch. To watch as it turns cold, stiffens. To see it distorted into death from vital flesh. To see blood flowing. To see the brains boiling over from the shattered skull. To see the bones unravelled from their seams.

And to watch as it is pushed into the earth or it rises in flames or is fed to vultures. Or, placed under some miraculous tree, wrapped in its bark, because here, flesh doesn't rot, but, perfuming the air, is soaked into the roots, so that you can see your loved one leaving little by little. Then there is comfort, then you weep, and even if you cannot cry, at least the business is complete, you finally realize he is gone, who was once yours.

But to vanish like this . . . how to believe in this death?

True that Ma had identified the pieces. Who knows how she sniffed out the whole story based on button and thread and ash. And so the government declared the case closed. But did Ma?

Watch her secretly and it shows. I watch her. The doorbell rings, and she jumps a little. A spark flashes in the dead-fish eyes.

This sort of ring? Where the finger stays on the bell endlessly? Youthful impatience. *Mom . . . open, quick.* Who . . .?

Something sparks in Ma's dead eyes and spreads slowly. Then it's gone. Dead fish. *Ab yahan koi nahin, koi nahin aayega.*

No one will come here ever again, never again . . .

But here is where he lives still. In every season Ma fills the bowl with his favourite fruit. The desserts he loved, she brings to me. Worried that I don't eat on my own. Worried that I don't speak. Worried that if a morsel is put into my mouth, I don't chew. Silent, I'm just silent. Tongue glued to mouth. Why?

Why, Ma asks. Don't you ever feel hungry? What are you thinking? What will you become, my child? Pilot, guitarist, tennis player, philosopher?

I'm no aviator, I don't fly planes. I don't play the guitar. I don't play tennis. I don't philosophize.

I am about nothing. I am not. Whether there is silence around me or noise, I don't care. Bombs explode, far and near, the newspapers renewing memories each time. Do whatever you want without me, listen if you want, leave me alone. Why shouldn't my tongue cleave to my palate?

Doing nothing, saying nothing, not moving my mouth, not chewing with my teeth; if I could help it, not growing an inch—these are my activities. This is my strength.

Ma has been given a goal. *Open your mouth.* Lovingly, fed up, threateningly. *Open your mouth.* Fretting, angry, hating me. *Open your mouth, my child.* Defeated.

The doctors are defeated too, but don't give up. Surgery would do it. Just a nick at the point where the tongue is stuck to the palate. *The circumstances of his birth . . . the fire in the cafe . . . difficult to say what . . .* they remind her with meaningful looks.

Ma stares, frightened. She starts forcing food into my mouth, morsel upon morsel. *Won't speak? Won't eat? We'll see.* Everything outside of her, machine-like. Must run smoothly. Does she fear that otherwise her inside, which is inside her now, will spill out?

I'll keep storing against my palate what is forced inside. But even my spit doesn't flow at my command. The slushy pushed in food keeps dangling. Like stalactites.

Chew, Ma commands. Drags me upright by force. Pushes my head back so that the food will be forced to go down. It slides, slides, slides down and then like a bomb it explodes on to Ma's face, in gobs, in smithereens.

The boy in the picture bursts out laughing. Ma, startled, looks around wildly. Here. There. Searching for her son.

Any mother would do this. Any father.

Search for their son, keep on searching, he could be anywhere, even now, anywhere . . .

18

Caps. Topis.

Call it a topi but caps are not just caps. Turbans, pagris, fez caps, topis, you name it, each can be the sign of a community. Some such piece of cloth—let's say a topi—the people of the community clapped on to Father's head, and mine, too.

Life has its upside down ways. Father never spoke to me, never did anything with me, but he did take me along to the meeting of the community.

Ma dresses me. Because I can't even dress myself. Can't button my shirt or buckle a belt. Teachers, neighbours, doctors—everyone advises Ma to send me to different kinds of places; I was bound to pick up some skill, learn something from somewhere. Ma sends me along, so I would be forced to learn, to this meeting, to any meeting, to school, to a stadium, with this person, with that, to a game. Because she wants me to whirr along in the machinery of the world like an efficient little wheel, go whirring along, somehow, just somehow; I should know that this is how I should whir along, whir, whir, fully into it, somehow, anyhow.

Everyone at the meeting alert, attentive. Here too, cameras, leaders, chairs, stage. The stage imbued with a magic of its own. Standing upon it, even Father begins to speak in a new voice, bubbling along like a stream, leaping over sands, pebbles, stones. And over me.

We were seated before his photograph, both of us topi-clad. And Father hurtled down at top speed between the fragments of himself suspended in space.

Says he, 'There is injustice and tyranny everywhere in the world. Ivory Coast, Peru, Rwanda, the Congo, Bali, Iraq, China, India, Afghanistan, Kosovo, Ukraine, Taiwan. And the so-called First World, expert in igniting fires, while all the time pretending to be Pope John Paul and Mother Teresa combined. But it was Hitler who was their progeny, born out of what they claimed were times of progress and awakening. Look how they continue to produce Hitlers indiscriminately. But cunning as they are, they don't permit today's Hitlers to assume the colour of their own faces, so that they can scream loudly and indignantly about the evil in other races.'

'Themselves safe in their fortresses,' he continues, 'they throw the rest of us into the mouth of cannons. Their own are safe. Others besieged by bombs. Who will die, who will survive, isn't it obvious?'

Looks at me, looks at him.

'Innocents die, the crafty survive.'

There's a spark in the eyes in the picture—a hero's eyes, of course there's a spark.

'Eighteen years.' Father's hold on the microphone tightens.

'What can anyone have accomplished in eighteen years? He was to have begun doing it all now.'

The earthquake in his voice, would the mike be able to take it?

'Where is light? What is our hope?'

Father falls silent. Everyone's loving eyes on the picture.

Mine too. Poor chap. My pal, after all. We live together, after all. There, in the place where he should have been. Doing what I am able to.

'Read the papers everyday,' Father says brokenly. 'One more son. One's child is a candle, mild in its sweet and tender glow. How can we allow it to be quenched? And look,' says Father suddenly remembering, 'do you know what his name means? The light at the end of the tunnel.' With pride he said, 'I had forgotten, it was he who reminded me one day, while studying our ancient language, this was what it meant. Oh, he was cut out to be a great scholar.'

Father stopped and swept an enquiring look over the assembly. Did his words have an impact? They had to.

Lots of caps are nodding. Of the old and the wise, too. Yes, true, he was indeed the light at the end of the tunnel.

'Yes, he reminded me,' Father repeated, and the light glowing at the end of the tunnel showered over the hall.

The clapping begins. 'Clap,' I was nudged.

The leaders take the mike from Father. 'True,' they say, 'true. What a darkness, but this darkness is not yours alone. It is an attack on our community. The candlelight is for all of us. We stand together and he stands with us. There is indeed, light at the end of the tunnel. Well said.'

Love and more love pouring from the stage towards the audience. Where was it to go, that light at the end of the tunnel, to whom should it give its brilliance? That love, that thwarted intensity, the overflowing energy of an eighteen-year-old, where should it be released?

19

Wise old folk and the people.
So here's my take on this.

Every era has its share of wise men. They are represented as sages, ancient overgrown trees, with cascading beards and deep, reflective, peaceful, sad, loving eyes.

But this is a fallacy. Wisdom has nothing to do with age. And age has nothing to do with being ancient.

Listen to these ancients with care. Their words resonate with significance. They possess the wisdom of the ages. Their meditation is eternal.

But this too is a fallacy. They have nothing to do with the ages. In fact they have nothing to do with wisdom.

We have mixed up everything. Some eras do that. Knowledge, meditation, generations, conventions, intelligence, essences. Listen to me, listen well. Information is not knowledge and knowledge is not vision. Vision comes from the judgement of experience, which comes from intelligence, which comes from the senses tactile, not from the brain, and intelligence is of three kinds: depraved, sagacious and witless.

What I'm saying is that wise men reflect their era. Their cascading beards, their sad eyes, match those of their era.

He and I are the wise old men of this era. One deep drag and we swoon endlessly into the smoke. Whether three or eighteen, we are the same age. Listening silently, watching quietly, saying much without speaking, feeling sad, so sad, at the world slipping from our grasp, standing on the edges of life and watching others struggling in midstream, remaining in that empty space where anything can happen, but will it?

And people? Those who are to listen to the ancients? They are neither depraved nor sagacious, nor are they witless. They are just pure-bred in their lack of intelligence, crass. Who think that those old trees are the wise ones, that mere movement is action, and meaning is where words are.

But not really. The great, the old, stories, action, are all elsewhere. Behind movement, hidden by words. Meandering amongst the pieces strewn in the galaxy. Were the pieces to join, you would get one whole human. If never joined, they will turn the entire galaxy brittle. A fine spray of dust will shower down in the form of red ants, spreading over my body in a painful rash, till I long to snuggle into the cool depths of some box, protecting what is left of me, so that no one may hurt me again.

20

And have you any idea what I'm talking about? But no, why should you? What do you have to do with death? But death is not a concern only for those who have died, my dear girl, died and gone to heaven or hell or some third place, but also for those who, seeing their beloved slide into death, circle round and round helplessly, at the edge of leaping in themselves—perhaps they can drag him out?

Because understand if you can, that death is a flood. And when a flood bursts out at any odd, unpredictable moment, like after a bomb, the living get embroiled with the dead in such a way that they forget that the two, the dead and the living, are two different species. The one who has gone is a fish perhaps, and we are monkeys. We leap up and climb trees and keep dragging the fish up into the branches, snare him in a photo frame, clap a topi on his head, bathe him in candlelight, assign him the age he would have been today, we bring the dead one alive time after time, only to kill him again.

Neither of us, my pal or I, can understand what you're up to, putting this cap on our heads and as for the candle, I refuse to blow it out, but I nibble just a bit of the cake.

'Let's go,' says Father to me, after the meeting is over. 'See what a large family he has given us,' he says to those assembled.

Someone tries to give me a toffee, and father says, 'He spits everything out, doesn't eat anything, don't worry.' Taking my hand he says, 'I'll get him a balloon-shaloon from the market.'

We come out of the meeting, amidst all those whisperings that mount up larger than my life. *That one is this, this one is that.* I cower by my father, without touching him. He's still holding my hand.

Once we're outside, he lets go of it.

Lost in his galaxy again. The balloon forgotten. It's forgotten, isn't it?

Apprehensive, I look at the shops. They may have balloons, but at least those will be sealed into packets, all shrivelled, not blown out.

I steal another look at Father. Hopefully he's forgotten the balloon plan.

The market is brilliant with lights. The sun has set, and the market has come alive. Dark days, shining nights.

The fun of being a speck lost in the dazzle of the market. A speck of darkness invisible amongst the sparkling lights. People don't notice you when there are shop windows to stare at. Objects in those windows draw their gaze like magnets. They stroll, their eyes fixed, spellbound. *Oh is that American model available here now? And see, that's a tribal design—you'll find it in the homes of all the posh people.*

Through all this bustle I walk in my depths, invisible in my darkness. My eyes turned inward, but swivelling outwards now and then, to make sure no balloon makes a sudden appearance, dancing anywhere in the air, round, swelling still, ready to burst.

That is how I remain, inside myself. Hidden away inside is all my crying, all my laughing, all my speaking, deep inside, so deep that by the time they make their way to the surface, their moment has passed.

Lifeless, stoic. Buddha-like.

Forging ahead, that image always with me. A round something lying forgotten in a corner, the rest is empty, emptiness; emptiness; the round thing lies desirous, gluttonous, coveting the sprawling empty space . . . why should it be so empty, how dare it lie empty . . . why shouldn't I roll in, roll in and burst and fly apart in all directions like flags and festoons and balloons at a fair.

Fearful, hopeful. The two feelings collide and I stumble into Father. Fall in the mud. A car goes honking past angrily.

'Why don't you look where you're going,' Father scolds. Because I fell on him? Or because I was saved from the car?

He does not say.

Saved. Once again, saved. Again and again I am saved.

21

That's why I charged to the door on reaching home. Kept my finger pressed to the doorbell, like he used to.

Would Ma have been startled? Would she have leapt to the door? Seeing me outside, would she have been confused?

You? She must have said.

Who else? Would I have said that?

Who knows, who remembers exact conversations time after time? Who remembers what escaped the lips, what remained pent up inside.

Who keeps count of how many lands slide, how many trees wither, how many drops of water never reach our rivers . . . who the hell keeps count?

And would he never have been startled and fallen into the mud? Is it just me who is human and fallible? Could I have burst out with that question when I heard Father say, 'He can't even watch where he's going. Wash him up.'

That's all he said about the meeting we were coming from, and Ma never asked for more.

Discussions over last rites had not yet begun and the box with him in it, with my friend in it, lay safely in Ma's locker.

A fish my friend, you agree? I say to her who has entered my story.

Ma lifted me to her lap. Despairingly. She removed my topi and placed it near the phone. Father turned away, not interested in dressing or undressing me, and as for me, I did nothing for myself, a stuffed toy at the meeting, so too at home.

Ma's voice came from far away inside. Entangled in memories of someone else. Wherever she was, she was certainly not with me, cradling my head in the soft inside of her neck as she drifted.

She took me to my room and went away. I lay down, on his bed, surrounded by the colours he chose, lay there dirtying his blanket. The picture on the wall had turned sombre, staring at me.

I stared back. For an instant, in one momentous space, we had been together. Since that instant, we have both been silent, whether wearing a cap or not!

Oh you're lying down, Ma came in with hot water, pulled the blanket away from me and began taking off my clothes. Carefully, avoiding the rashes. Gently, crying out over them as if they were hurting her, 'Every day I shake the sheets out, how do you call them back again, these ants?'

She wet a towel with hot water, wrung it out and sponged me. I shut my eyes as if it was me who lay in that box and felt Ma's caresses, soft on my pieces.

The windows in the room remain shut. I want to stay inside the box.

'You'll have to eat,' Ma says, bringing me food. She still feeds me. *One has to eat,* she teaches me the ways of life. *It even begins to taste good.* An accusation, a comforting. *You have to speak. One must speak. One must do everything.* It's a threat now. *And you have to do it well.* Some do it till they're eighteen, some have to keep on doing it. *All that he did, and all that he could not do.*

That voice pulls me out of the box. We must not cry, my look tells her.

How you look at me . . . something . . .something in your eyes . . . like in his . . . you're looking at me exactly like . . .

Exactly like the one who stares at me and at whom I stare back in the solitude of our room.

22

This is what I want to tell you, yes, exactly this, I said to her who was soon to enter this story or whatever it is, I want to tell you, yes. I want to tell you everything, I look at you with grateful eyes, see. There is so much to tell if I ever get to the telling. And there's nothing strange about this because it's true of everyone's life that if they start talking, they talk endlessly.

But you are listening, aren't you, I draw her gaze away from the photograph to me; let me also tell you there are ways and ways of being talkative. Some are talkative by talking, while others—I, coming from my empty space; Ma, sinking in her dead eye-sockets; Father, scattered in the ether; and him, the whole one, so charming, with his pieces enclosed in a box—we all talk endlessly in our silence. Chitter-chatter chitter-chatter, tirelessly, under our quiet skins, our fragments speak. We look like we are *here*, in our quietness, but actually we are *there*, making a hell of a racket. Diving into yesterday. The yesterday that is gone. The Past.

P-A-S-T. Mouthing it, the lips hang heavy from the face, heavy, so heavy . . . P-A-S-T!

She listened encouragingly as I sermonized away like a wise ancient. How light the word for today. P-r-e-s-e-n-t. There. It has slid out before you know it.

In the present, the day dawns, and where it dawns first is the land of the rising sun. The call of the muezzin, bells, the cock crowing, prabhatpheri, the tinkling of bells. Reluctantly, the sun rises. In the parks, yoga, taichi, laughing clubs. School buses and garbage trucks obstruct the roads. Carts and baskets, fruits and vegetables, fish and milk, saws and drills, walls absorbing the rays of the sun, all joining the race to beat the day. This boring present, dry with grey, grey dreams.

But the past? Full, heavy. Stoked with gunpowder. At the slightest nudge, fountains burst forth, fire spews, I said, and sawdust rains down on today. It flies out of that heavy past, on the winds of today, to settle like a pall of dust, to spread over the towns, to paint in grey, grey, all the dreams and seeds and fruits and flowers and bees, to wither the wings of the birds, grey *grey* in one sweeping stroke, this past, this past, damn this past!

The past when it barges into the present shifts life from its centre. The axis shifts to one side and we with it. Our present lurches on its pivot and we topple into that which is gone . . .

On and on I gushed, in a torrent, after years of silence. Inching back out from the margins along with my past.

Look how I open up to you, I murmur like an intoxicated lover. Oh. So much. Every bit of me, my entire being. Like a woman? Like you? I look at her playfully. She was making me flirtatious. I just want to burst, see, I say. Like a dam.

Like a bomb, she teased, naughtily. I'm making her naughty! Yes, exactly like a bomb, actually.

When the bomb dropped on Hiroshima, there was a man sitting on the steps outside a bank waiting for it to open so that he could go in and do his work. How could he have known that it was somewhere else he would go? Did he ever know? No. He just went up in smoke and it was the rest of the world that knew. Even today, in the Hiroshima museum you can see those steps, an abstract artwork in black, on which, listen, there is an empty space, a space that did not burn because he sat there to save it. He, who became one with the air.

Is that how an empty space gets left behind? Does the one left in it manage to save a tiny bit of room in a devastated world? The air rising from that empty space hides in itself some dream . . . some seed . . . a glow? Some clue to lead to something . . . someone . . . Or is there anyone . . .?

23

Children grow up. The living as well as the dead. Darkness parts by itself and the sun glows red. All humming with life, grain in the fields, water in the rivers, snow on the peaks, young ones on the roads, bells on bicycles, snuggling in bed, your spirit sings. Then must you roll in the grass, sway to the rhythm of falling leaves, stuff pakauri after pakauri into your mouth, for which Ma scolds you, enough, no more, those are for the kadhi, leave them alone, and you yell so loudly that Father comes running and joins in too, gobbling up pakauris with the son, and infectious laughter wells up in Ma and Father and son, in that happy little town that exists now only inside the heart.

When people from the community drop in, or schoolmates or friends from his band, then Father talks as if the son who has gone is still there in their midst, chattering fluently like them.

While the son who is actually here, is not there in this huge-big-family-that-he-has-given-us!

'You youngsters are so argumentative,' Father says to his friends but he's back in time with him, and is laughing with great gusto but with a thin sliver of panic in there too, fearful of snapping out of the moment if he stops.

Those present in the room too, don't want such moments to snap. They feel a surge of compassion in their hearts. Their words intertwine with Father's words, forming threads which they weave into a silken wrap around the moment.

One of his alert friends laughs loudly. A little too loudly. A laughter reflecting the terror that the silken wrap may not hold.

'So if we don't agree with you we're argumentative!'

'Not at all,' says Father.

'Long live democratic dissent—long live! Zindabad!' The boys chant teasingly. 'Death to authoritarian consensus—death to it! *Murdabad* . . .' They stop aghast, the familiar slogan suddenly too literal on their lips.

'Silenced you, haven't I?' Father is victorious at the defeat of the friends.

Once again another meaning lashes out at the gathering. Slowly the conversation flows again, words chosen with care so that they don't appear in their old implications.

Father goes on and on, loud and dramatic, so that memories remain at bay.

Ma lost in her tea and pakauris, I lost on the stairs, Father lost among his dead son's friends.

These visitors will have to leave sometime. Words in their sharpness will try to pull apart the satiny seams of the silken wrap. The town inside will begin to be extinguished. Seeing it descend into darkness, Father will be terrified and rush with the used dishes to the kitchen.

Ma's back is towards him. The body of a woman. Or is it? Father touches her. His hand slides down the woman's back.

Perhaps some sensation will return, perhaps the pieces will come together? But he can feel nothing. Anxious hands search her waist, her breasts, her crotch. Ma turns to him. Her eyes glassy and full of hurt like those of an injured animal. Something bursts aflame in them, the embers fly to her irises and then vanish into darkness.

Nothing joins up, no shiver rises, hands keep sliding up and down a body as if lost in the act of dying, bit by bit, grain by grain, sliver by sliver, keep dying, lost on that body going numb. Nothing remains. Except for a small piece of meat between Father's legs, indifferent to him, to his pieces, to his motives, growing in the town like a cancer.

Meanwhile in that town which lay outside, what we called morning was an ashen, grey, lustreless sun climbing the sky.

24

From that ashen sun come the proverbs and sayings of this town, this era; from it come their wise folk. Where a lie is uncovered to expose, not the truth, but another lie. A lie that he is alive and a lie that he is dead. And I too!

Startled, Ma and Father's eyes dart towards any familiar trait—a walk, a turn of the head—as if every bird is one bird because they all have wings.

Because at the moment they accept his death he will have to be resurrected, they will nurture the lie that he is alive. The parents will stop trying to work out this puzzle and continue to live lie upon lie upon lie.

Or truth upon truth upon truth.

Truth is lie in this era, so twisted that they are indistinguishable and inside this twistedness will run the rest of our lives, Ma's and Father's and mine and his. Studded on the walls he will watch the non-stop rehearsal of his life.

He stands firm and tall and well muscled. Behind the glass lie full-bodied possibilities.

Silently pleading, *let me come down or else let me go.*

Because whether he spoke or not, and I spoke or not, or spoke just as much as I had begun, sometimes, a little, to speak, or kept my tongue locked up like his in his box, even then I can see that this house is a cave.

In caves, lights only deepen the darkness. If you frolic about in caves, the shadows become ghosts and ogres dancing on the walls. Inside caves, the dead and alive swap roles. The eyes of the living turn inwards and up and the tongues of those in photo frames start wagging. Yes and no merge in such a manner that there is a picture on this side of the glass, and on that side of course, and each side nurses the illusion that the other is the photo!

Watching quietly. Slowly sliding backwards. Hiding, popping out, this is what happens in a cave.

You grow quietly, very secretly, your ages and identity mixed up. You keep growing without eating, without speaking. At four you're also nineteen and at twenty, you're five too; at six, twenty-one, when seven, twenty-two. At eight you can count twenty-three on your fingers. Twenty-four means nine. Twenty-five turns ten and at eleven you shoot up like a palm tree. At twelve I feel so old. At twenty-seven he stays only eighteen in the photograph. At thirteen it gets increasingly difficult for me to clench my mouth shut and remain the lump of flesh lying among ants. At twenty-nine I am still a gawky fourteen. And at fifteen you immediately recognize the sounds in the cave that have been around you for thirty years. Almost at once, at the slightest stir you know that Ma has once again opened her metal cupboard and touched again, the box in her locker.

25

Missing persons. At home, but gone missing. Baffled about their own whereabouts. Who, where, why, the more questions you ask, the more lost they get. Sir, you must give us some hint, some clue, how else are we to return you to where you belong? Tell us the *a b c* of your name, the *ka kha ga* of your job, and leave the rest to us. So then, kind sir, please begin.

Missing persons. Sort of floating. Emitting not speech but bubbles of air. Name? '*Father*' *maybe. Or* '*Ma*'. Address? *Somewhere near our son.* Work? *Work . . . well, you could call it a sort of small business; we have taken on a contract to protect our son.*

Oh come on, how do you expect us to help you? This work, it's what everyone does. Useful clue this, like saying we live by the sea and under the sky!

Missing people like these. Us. Together, alone. Maybe it happened right then.

When the bomb exploded.

When that moment froze in time. That moment became life. That moment became meaning. The rest, oblivion.

And somehow to live out what remains. Days of stupor. Nights. Until one day the missing persons are no more, then there will be no more the missing.

Like deflated balloons waiting for air, the missing people. Another day and the same headlines. An explosion, some blown into the air, others hurled to the ground.

We see the headlines but we don't talk about it, and yet some air enters the balloons. The doorbell will ring today. School friends will arrive. Folks from the community. The sarvadharmasabha people will show their faces. It will occur to some new ones to turn up. Reporters, researchers, many an interested and sympathetic character will pull up at the door. What-a-big-family-he-has-given-us, and how it flourishes.

I am in his pyjamas and Ma is coaxing me to eat a seed-filled fruit that he loved. She says, in any case you can't eat more than a piece or two, the seeds can give you a tummy ache, so come on, just one piece.

Even my tummy should be like his and start aching when I eat the seeds!

I take the fruit into my mouth and then forget. Lost as usual. Ma slaps me lightly on my cheek. *Such a big boy now and still cannot eat by himself. What a face—like a toothless old man! Take it to the side, come on now, to the side, and then chew with your teeth.*

The doorbell rings. The balloons begin to inflate. His friends arrive with the fish he loved so that Ma can cook it for them.

To remember him with love and to be happy, as he would have wanted.

'Hey, aren't you watching World Cup Soccer!' they say to

Father and turn on the television.

To turn him away from his memories, and from his sadness. Remembering brings him to mind, and not remembering does too. Running into a bomb does this to you. A single nudge and the memories start rolling in. In they come and refuse to leave. Even when they leave, they have not gone, they remain all spread out, wispily.

Because the world is huge and bombs are of many kinds. Fill a bottle with water and freeze it, that's a bomb. Pack sulphur in a beer can, a bomb. Nano bomb, dirty bomb, atom bomb, cluster bomb, how many names? Smoke bombs, RDX, and balloon bombs called fugos. These are silk balloons, filled with hydrogen, a hundred feet in radius, come floating down on a parachute, attracting picnicking children who run towards it to play with it, and it plays with them instead.

And it's well known that there are explosives called dumb bombs. Honestly, that's what they're called. But this I do say: anything dumb is also innocent. Someone else gives me a shove, and off I go: Look at me, I'm a bomb, I'm a bomb! My weight is 113 kilos. But soaring easily in flight I can sweep over several football and cricket fields at one go. So innocent. Daisy Cutter is my name. Keep at it you scientists, do what you will, try laser or missile or nuclear techniques to turn me smart, but dumb I am, dumb I shall remain. As the old song goes, '*kahin pe nigahen, kahin pe nishaana, kaisa yeh kaisa, deewana hai zamaana!*' Sometimes like the sweet simpleton I am, I might win, but quite often I lose. I'm dumb. Set out to kill someone and they don't get killed, and sometimes setting out to explode, but failing to.

Do you get it? Do you, my girl? It means that we have spread out all over the world, innocent, unsuccessful bombs, some under the earth, some in balloons, some looking like airdropped medicine or food packets; all unknowing the bomb, but one foot towards it, or hand, or laughter, and everything evaporates.

There's more. While we are at it, think also of those who are human bombs that have not managed to explode. Yet . . .

26

It's hardly then a matter of great surprise where so many disappear and a few get left behind, that friends and well-wishers should gather together in camaraderie. Call it a bomb party if you will. New recipes, delightful new ways of serving. The bomb.

Not that the bomb looks like a bomb in every dish. Pulav, kheer, papad, dosa. You have to be pretty astute to make out.

But then don't think of the bomb as just a bomb, either. A big bomb might be crude, a smaller one, the latest. The bomb is Einstein and knowledge, progress and electricity, it is water, harvest, grain. The bomb is the nation's border, the bomb is a superpower, the bomb is a buffoon. It shatters the earth, it pierces the sky. It terrifies, but oh, look at its terrible beauty. Who sets off bombs? Men, women, educated, illiterate, rustic, computer wizards, kings, gods, demons, communalists, nationalists, dreamers, pessimists, foreigners, natives, touchables, untouchables, apes, bulls, I or anyone else—who can tell, who knows these things and who talks of them; the bomb was waiting forgotten, in that heavy, heavy past, the rest was just empty space and the present that is lost; the today that had stopped still, stopped, waiting to be drawn into the ring of fire, hoping—*maybe I too can be blown to smithereens, I too can become meaningful.*

The talk circled around and about the headlines and there were so many bombs and so many speeches and behind it all, silent, but not hidden, there he was. The one in pieces. The one in the pictures.

And when do we begin to make sense of all this, Father was going on and on, quite beside himself, *it follows no order, no chronology, no logic of place or time, after all, when will it all make sense . . .*

All what, I would have asked, if I used to speak then.

When your child who was the pride of the community . . .

The community? Whose community . . . how . . . I would have asked, had I spoken at the time.

He offered up himself. My beautiful, charming son whose future became the sacrificial offering for the nation, for community, for world peace.

The photograph beckoned, I saw. His glowing face seemed to be listening uncomprehending, as if we were talking in a tongue unknown.

Ma called me. I went. She got me busy in something or the other; as if to convey her irritation—why was I listening furtively to their conversation, and why would I not listen to her? Listen that is, to what she was whispering angrily. A bolt of lightning in her eyes so that for a moment the fish began to swim. *Did anyone actually see him in the cafe, you were there, was he there, did you see him, and all those who were injured, were they all identified, and did anyone trace those who recovered from their injuries and went away without being identified, and did anyone actually see his body disappear, as if someone could just vanish like that. Iron, his body was iron, wouldn't I know, I, his mother . . .?*

She smiled. Sitting me on her lap. Holding my face in her hands and looking carefully at me. When the fish stopped swimming she turned my face to her shoulder and started rocking me to sleep. Murmuring in my ears, 'Did anyone see what there was in that box? It was sealed. There was nothing in it. It was empty. That's why he has had no last rites.'

I felt the darkness and Ma was smiling. Ma was smiling on and on.

27

Of course, it's true, about the last rites. All those clippings of interviews say this, that in the family of the bombed son, the box is safe, still locked up in Ma's cupboard. Ma doesn't talk about it and refuses to pull it out for the cameras. Father though, is beginning to take seriously the community's suggestion that the box be bid a proper farewell with all appropriate rites. I am silent and the clippings say it is natural he should be timid and scared, but Ma, catching me alone says, *but you aren't, are you*, and actually I'm not, it's just that I am deep inside myself and take a long time to come to the surface, and the world has no patience and *what a nuisance*, says Father but whether about me, or about me not speaking, I'm not sure, and he asks for the box.

They quarrel, Father and Ma.

Hearing them fight I retreat quietly up the stairs, sliding backwards till my head hits the wall. I keep pressing up against it like I'm bent upon being absorbed by the layers of whitewash.

We were wrong, says Father, never, neither at his birth, nor ever later—*nor ever later*, he says—to have done what had to be done, no rituals, no prayers.

So now the box should be drowned in ritual, that's what the quarrel is about, I begin to understand. I push my fingers hard into my temples, pressing my head back into the bricks. The blood in my veins begins to freeze.

Straighten the table, Ma's voice is icy. It's a goodbye voice. She has already said goodbye and when her voice is forced to appear, this is how it sounds.

That's how anyone would have been, I understand now, at a time when everything lay ahead. Such overwhelming pride as Father must have felt when the box-boy was born, such certainty that life lay gloriously ahead, that this was the golden boy of the future; intoxicated on his happiness and hope, he would have rejected all ritual, all rites as ignorant superstition. No holy water to be touched to the forehead, no divine flame to be absorbed through devout cupped palms. No rosary to tell, no special chants meant to be uttered over children. A luminous time, warm in its own glow, awaiting no prophet from elsewhere whose arrival was needed to launch the celebration. Not at his birth and not ever later.

Father said *not ever later.*

Ma did not say *not even at his death.* Because the act of flying into the air and just disappearing is not automatically accorded the status of death.

She just shook off Father's voice as she had shaken off his hand and turned her gaze to the pictures on the walls. The golden boy of the future. Smiling lovingly down at her, calm, unworried.

My head felt numb, so hard had I pressed it against the wall. Hidden, I continued listening. He listened too, from the pictures, understanding something, perhaps not understanding.

Slowly I began to relax my head, as if to separate its identity from the wall. The blood that had stopped flowing, leapt up and started running in my veins. I felt something snaking round the darkness inside my head.

It was me myself, slipping, sliding.

28

Now listen to what happened. Nothing. Just that one more connection snapped. Between Father and Ma. Father walked down the stairs . . .

. . . and left forever the room he shared with Ma upstairs. He crossed an invisible line and Ravana abducted him. The study downstairs became his Ashok Vatika, the falling piles of papers and books, his trees and creepers, desolate, with no birds twittering; and the keys of the box remained with Ma, and Father's new occupation became going to prayer services week after week, and who knows for what reason, dragging me with him. Because he had stopped talking to Ma, and anyway, she wouldn't have gone? Or because he was scared to go alone? Or because he wanted to show me again and again, *look, look at his glory, his greatness, celebrated endlessly at these meetings*? So that I could go back and relay to Ma how important her son was?

Returning from work, straight into the study. This is his room now. Just lying there, lying there. When the food was laid out on the table he might sometimes, as if by mistake, or as if he had gathered up his courage in his hands, join Ma and me, eating silently. Or he would remain in his room, emerging only when we had finished. This became the pattern of our days of going missing now, of our endless wait.

But if you're willing, dear girl, I'll take you back to the day when we were to attend the prayer meeting, for then you'll see once again the days when that balloon was filled with air.

Father is dressed, and he has his cap on.

He does not need to say it but it is known that I must be ready too. I had begun to wear his watch, and had learnt to tell the time. Its dial has a calculator and also shows the time in all the important capitals of the world.

The imagined ringing of the doorbell is already filling the balloon with air. The bell rings and the balloon plumps out immediately. Now the balloon looks like a balloon. Not shrivelled up but round and full.

We step out with those who have come to fetch us. Once outside, Father hands me my cap and I paste it on my head.

The huge-big-family-he-has-given-us, is welcoming. Fragrance from incense and attar. The throng is one throbbing soul with many bodies and there is music and singing and enthusiasm and sorrow and solidarity and a rising, roaring, clamorous euphoria in which there is the father and there is the son and no one can separate them, no bomb, no gun, nothing can just blow them away as if they're nothing. No-o-o . . . the maddened voices ring out, roar, rise in crescendo. Drowning in tears. The grief so intense that it threatens to pounce on you and devour you. A hysterical pounding in each head, like a drum being hammered by someone up above.

Mine too? Or am I in my usual mode?

But look at Father, my girl. Shuddering in a trance so obsessive, impossible to tell the dancer from the dance. Does he know himself?

But he is with his son. The gathering has given his son back to him.

Naturally then, after the meeting when we come home and he heads for the study, the balloon began to deflate. His son is left behind in the hall and he is alone at the door of his house saying goodbye to those who have accompanied him.

Standing at the door after the goodbye, his face towards those departing, his back towards me. Slowly his back begins to wilt. I can see the air slipping out of him. Its descent visible. Slowly his spine hunches down. Downwards the shrivelling spreads to his limbs, to his knees, his legs, his feet, the balloon emptying out. Just a little air left in the feet. He must use it to walk very carefully.

Father turns. Staggers. His feet keep moving with difficulty, dragging his wilted body.

Barely manages to enter his room before he collapses.

You see what I'm showing you? I ask her.

29

You see what I'm showing you, I ask her—she who will come, will certainly come, otherwise how will I speak, after all, there is life in me—or something like life—it's I, the empty space that wants to wail, *listen, listen*, dying to speak, dying to speak.

You see? I ask her. His dying? Drop by drop, limb by limb, till nothing was left. I burst out laughing and she covers her face with her hands. I'm not laughing, I assure her, *don't be scared, but that golden boy of the future killed him.*

She shakes her head vigorously, disagreeing.

Yes, yes. I insist. That golden boy of the future is the black boy of the past and the murderer of the present.

In bits, Father goes away to die. Only every now and then, that which lies between his legs wakes up with a jerk at his touch like it were something lost that has stumbled in from outside, from outside his body even, a last surviving piece hinting at his self, at his *I,* and in desperation he would try to produce from it, somehow, a tremor.

But do they ever add up, out there in space, a tremor here and a tremor there? Can they join up to make a whole human?

The slightest movement and that orphaned little thing would shrivel up again.

30

One should bid the final farewell.

Otherwise you end up like Father. Yearning, always yearning, for the kindling of some spark, for the trembling of something into life, for the means to carry on living.

Ma has bid farewell. She has said goodbye to herself. She has gone away to some place where her son is. The rest of the world is but a moment of waiting.

Listen. Let me say something about waiting.

Everyone waits. Both the dead and the living. The dead wait to live again and the living call out impatiently to death.

Also . . .

In everyone's life there is an event so momentous that it freezes memory inside itself forever, so that nothing remains outside its shape and colour and melody, nothing else is understood, nothing else awaited.

Like . . .

There was a jungle, the hunger of whose human inhabitants grew and grew, their desire for flesh became so overpowering that they decided to eat the animals living with them in the jungle. But when the humans turned to them, weapons upraised, licking their lips greedily, the animals, their companions, spoke up and said, *Don't kill us, oh don't kill us, we are one community, after all.* So the humans performed austerities to please the gods, a period of austerities that was a form of waiting, so that the animals living with them should forget the language they all shared. Do you know what happened then? The humans raised their hands to slaughter and the animals turned their gaze towards them, but at that very moment the language they had shared until then fled their memories, and the animals bent their necks in submission.

Since then the natives of that jungle lie in wait to kill the animals and the animals await the rubbing of salt and pepper into their flesh.

Because . . .

In each one's life some such thing happens that becomes forever his destiny and forever then he is in waiting for it.

Then hear this too. That never again . . .

Will you be freed from this waiting. Or let's say the waiting remains inside you, absorbed in its toilette. Face pack, massage, manicure, pedicure, preparing itself to glow. Glowing, to leap out and attack you. Biding its time to go straight for your throat. Again and again. Time after time.

While you, poor fool, all unknowing, keep yourself busy imitating life.

Idiot! You don't realize that this—the waiting—is your caretaker now, your sentinel, your light, your parents, your kith and kin, your child, the music in your blood, the desire in your empty spaces, the bolt that can destroy you, the bomb that can set you aglow; think about it, I'm not wrong. I am a wise one of this jungle, and so is he and he would have said the same, if he could have spoken, from the box or from the photograph.

It's worth thinking about. That grief can create worlds, and destruction too. So can a bomb. And what happens once has to happen again and again. Less than that, and how will I feel it in my very skin? Less than that, and it may as well not have happened.

That is why . . .

Again and again I will run towards it, even if I am trying to run away from it. It's all I have now, it's my simile, synonym, noun, proverb, verb, it's my sun, moon, star, thirst and seasoning.

You don't get it? Oh my innocent girl, the bomb becomes my language and my very breath.

Something happens at some point in life, before birth or death, or afterwards, or somewhere in between, and once it has happened, it becomes our language and we cannot but pour ourselves into it and flow with it.

My palms are aflame, my eyes and my lips, and I am wild with longing to set her on fire with them.

So this, I tell her, is how I've been going on. On the outside, absorbed in normal activity, all the while hiding the bomb inside. All the time, in all the crowd, in all the quiet. Never for a moment have I forgotten it. Whatever the words on the page in front of me, all I can see before my eyes is b-o-m-b. No matter where I go, to a film, meeting, festival or party, the only word that form on my lips is b-o-m-b. Whatever anyone says, I want to reply b-o-m-b. Ma says, speak son, I want to say b-o-m-b.

Yes, language was forming inside, bubbling up from deep inside, and for a long time no one understood. Not even Ma.

What . . . what did you say . . . I heard something . . . yes, yes . . . speak beta . . . speak . . . you said 'mom' . . .

She gathered me into her lap and kissed me, 'Beta said, Mom.'

No, Beta did not say Mom. Beta said another word. It's bubbling up. B-o-m-b!

31

Winter clothes should be aired in the sun before the cold sets in. And when winter is over, they should be dry-cleaned and stored away for the next season. Even if the one who once wore them, now lives on the walls. But if during the winter the son staying in your house adds another year to his body, you can hang the other son's warm clothes on him. Just tuck in this seam, let out that one.

Measuring me in his measure. Ma was an expert at this.

When the education department decided to institute scholarships in the name of the children of the bomb families, this skill of Ma's came in handy. Measuring me, sixteen years old, measuring his three-piece suit, thirty-one years old. The slither of the measuring tape on my skin, stretching to his outline around my body. Reduce the suit by that much, and there I am.

Overnight, his suit made place for me. Next morning Ma got me dressed; his tie was tightened round my neck, and she gestured to me to go with Father.

Ma never went to these public gatherings.

Father stared as if he was seeing me in his clothes for the first time.

I don't think the bomb families cared much for each other's company. They wanted to be unique. Like their child was unique. The meeting went on and on, about the amount of the scholarship and the proposed ceremony, but nobody met anybody's eyes.

In a way our family was different, but that was hardly something Father was proud of. That when it came to the ceremony of handing out the scholarship, we were the only family that could do it with two hands, his and mine. Meaning they had me, if they wanted to acknowledge it. I mean, there I was, the only one to have overpowered the death-dealing bomb.

That empty space, don't refuse to own it, if for no other reason than the fact that it's the only failed part of the plot that eliminated your son.

But who will say this to Father?

Anyway, there are all these meetings and like a relay race, I am made to take over where he left off. If I refuse to run, well then, I'm just a bloody idiot, what can they do about it?

So my hands presented the envelope. Father blessed the awardee.

We sat on the stage. Father and I. Along with the picture of him and the pictures of the other sons.

The master of ceremonies touched my shoulder, would I like to speak?

'He does not speak,' said Father. Despairing? Adamant? That's all right. The man said kindly. No hurry. There's a

whole life ahead of you. You will bring honour to his name. He opened up the path for you. We're so proud . . .

'Say thank you,' Father nudged me.

He'll speak. He'll surely speak. The man reassured Father. He's growing up, he's acquiring skills. And you know, my wife was remembering just the other day that he was quiet too, your son, when he was small. Very observant and attentive, listening quietly to all that was going on around him, mulling over it no doubt, in his head. But he did begin to speak, didn't he? So will this one. He's just like him. Even his eyes . . .

Ma says that too. That something in my eyes is like his!

One of those days when Father wasn't home, she had pulled out her mobile phone and dialled the landline. She had just got it, the mobile.

The phone rang.

'Will you speak like him, beta?' she pleaded, hurrying me down the stairs, pressing the phone to my ears.

The voice came from some other world: 'You have reached . . .

we are not at home . . . please leave a message after the beep.' The voice of the photograph.

I left no message.

32

Meaning I kept quiet.

Everyone said of me, he is so quiet. So *chup-chup*.

So timid. This is he. The one who survived in the other one's place. Sit him down anywhere, dress him as you please.

I became used to it, to wear whatever muffler, belt, cap was put on me. All timid on the outside. But actually, timid? Me? Not a bit!

Careful was what I was.

Very careful. Hidden well inside my skin. Not a feather out of place.

Arrogant, you might think. But why should what I really feel be visible to all? When even exploding gunpowder was defeated by this skin, can mere expressions splinter it? I'm careful, not timid, and contained within myself. Like the bomb lying quietly in a corner.

And quiet I shall remain, try as you might.

Okay listen, about me and speaking. Or about being quiet. Quiet gathers in, speech scatters.

How unbearable those who talk too much. All that there is to them, is what they say. They talk, and we know them inside out. The more they talk the more they dissolve any desire in us to explore them deeply. That is, if such a desire had ever existed.

If. Then.

But what if they didn't speak? Remained quiet? Those people?

You could drown in them. Diving deeper, further and further away from the banks that kept you safe. If you had the courage.

If.

They say that in the depths of the ocean there are creatures whose address you'll find on no envelope. The Loch Ness monster and other animals you think are myths, one deep breath and in they suck everything on the surface of the water—whole ocean liners and giant birds in the sky and ships from other planets floating in space—like little toys, sucked right in. Not a trace of them left behind, not even their ghosts.

I can tell you more. Shall I? I bet you don't know that in the depths of the seas, where no light reaches, there are huge forests. Not of trees but of insects, several metres long, like white tubes with red wings. No light reaches them so you know what they do? They make their own electricity. Their heads glow at two to three degrees of heat, their feet at fifty. Silent lies the jungle and silent lies the bottom of the ocean.

Not the *bottom*, it's the *bottomless*.

Perhaps you know—yes, perhaps this you know—that under the seas there are volcanoes, spewing lava.

Bottomless.

So that's what I'm saying. Quiet is bottomless and where there is quiet there is energy and boiling lava. If you find quiet, you can dive in and die there. For in the desire to drown, hides the greed to live.

So isn't this what happened, when I saw you and you saw me? Didn't my silence draw you in? I know I'm talking a lot today, but that's different. Volcanoes, let them be for now.

So. We, who remain quiet, are mysterious, smoky, magical beings.

The speech of such people! Even in their speaking echoes a mysterious quiet, the murmuring of the unsaid, an absence lurking behind the spoken, some devastation behind everything made explicit, something inward-looking in each clarification.

This is the magnetic attraction of the bomb family. In their silence the photographs speak. In their daily chores, in their everyday words, murmurs the rhythm of a primordial poetry, of a bottomlessness where no light reaches, and people are startled, looking around wildly, where did that voice come from, did someone speak? Ma, Father, I, the photograph?

Silence, that's all there is here. Silent too, the box in the locker.

And yet . . .

33

One incident and that becomes my everything.

Tumhi ho mata pita tumhi ho! Tumhi ho bandhu sakha tumhi ho!

Thou art my Mother and my Father! Friend and companion thou art!

The incident that becomes the driver and keeper of the rest of my life. The incident that provides the metaphor thereafter for everything in my life. The same degree of pain, with the same severity, exactly the same has to happen, nothing less can happen, anything less is as if it has not happened, nothing has happened if *that* has not happened!

There is always proof, provided proof of the proof is not demanded. Our father. His child blown to pieces, and the wire connecting his pieces together, blown up too. Up flew the pieces, and up blew the connection. The desire to live, lurking sometimes in one piece and sometimes in another, which if they were joined together would make one full man.

Shall I tell you something? Something I've never said to anyone before. In any case, what do I say to anyone else? And what do I not say to you?

What is it about you, you get me started and then keep listening. Were you made just to listen to me? Am I something . . . someone . . .?

So this is what I knew—and Ma too—that Father and the woman . . .

I know that gaze of his. Breaking into pieces what he looks at. Slice by slice, limb by limb, like carving meat with a fork and knife.

A journalist and a researcher, a woman.

Ma knows. These days Father comes to the table to eat when she's there. He doesn't speak, but sometimes passes her a dish.

We who live up above. The one above knows everything!

A bomb has exploded. Vengeance is demanded. Those who were meant to die have died, those who were not meant to, have died too, and both have acquired the same colour, and both have become of one species.

'How do you feel when . . .'

'How did you feel when . . .'

'How are you feeling when . . .'

The tape recorder is switched on and the woman is open before him.

Bit by bit, father fills up with air. Under his feet the stage takes shape. On his head the cap has descended. He will speak and he will not stop.

How does it feel . . . when your son is blown up . . .

The woman's eyes shine. Before her, the hero. The superstar. The man in the amazing story. What will she not do for him.

Piece by piece, Father gets agitated. Above him, us. His shattered son.

'I can't sleep,' he declares.

The woman's eyes swim with tears.

'How does it *feel* . . .' Father repeats in contempt. Begins to speak. History, geography, political science, sociology, physics, chemistry. People, nation, caste, community, power, fanatics, progress.

Father is sort of shouting, weighed down by the pieces, unable to join them together, in growing fear that he will never be able to pull them together—where is his son in all of this, how to die himself, but how not to die . . .

Looking at the woman in front of him his grief turns to lust. The desire to die seeks to escape into life. He turns his eyes to the picture but lowers his gaze. It returns shamelessly to the woman.

'I'll never sleep again.'

Ma shuts the door. Father needs the warmth of a woman's body. He has declared it: he is helpless, desperate, he will never sleep otherwise.

I just lie there on the stairs.

For some time then this woman would keep coming, go into father's room, Ma would close the door, giving Father permission, if you can't sleep otherwise, here, sleep. Father would wait. A shameless throb would arise in a part outside of him, never touching his inside. All he had to do was speak and see the woman melt and inside him would grow his irritation, that she thought she could understand. How does one feel . . .!

His words were neither true nor false or were both, and they were like ropes to knot her with. And there she was, in his lap.

In his anger, he played with her like she was the galaxy where the pieces he had lost were strewn. Grab a fistful. Some more in a mouthful.

The woman would scream. *Really, it hurts!* Her eyes hurt. Her body.

'Good,' Father would laugh. *It should hurt.* 'Child,' he would say to her, lifting a tear with the tip of his tongue, and just as she was beguiled by his gentleness, he would pounce again, spit out the tears, and rip her with his teeth.

Only in this way could he feel. By breaking her. Bit by bit. Taking care not to shatter her completely. He is terrified of the power of shattering. But to shatter just a little. To remain in control. So that he can keep forgetting. His son. The woman too. The ones above.

Shameless desire. Contempt is what stirs his lust. Hell and heaven in one small piece. That belongs neither to his soul, nor really to his body. Just flares up like a matchstick and then dies out.

Father gave nothing and got nothing. He was left in tatters yet again. One small bit of his body had imitated the act of living, but life itself remained impotent, just impotent.

34

Silent, the air. As if all is forgotten. The present most of all. The past has gobbled up all sound. What is left in the present is no bomb, just a balloon.

I'm sidling up to the house, trying not to be seen. Turn the key in the lock.

Fuck, it's bolted from inside. Will have to ring the bell. And face that oh-it's-*you* look from whoever opens the door.

My hand on the doorbell. My strong square wrist. Like his, Ma says.

She knows how to track down on my body and in my mind, similarities with him. After all, both have two ears, two eyes, one cock, many silences.

Had the bomb taken an eye of mine or a leg, would Ma not have seen me at all? Perhaps I would have been lying where I was. She might not have brought me home.

But now it's all right, I'm looking at my wrist. He was a member of the rowing club and went rock climbing and I don't play tennis but this wrist is okay, it will do!

My age too follows in his footsteps—from three to four, then five, then six and so on, and today I am seventeen.

Father does not open the front door for me.

But I have to go past his door. There hasn't been a blast anywhere, no woman has been coming to interview him, and the door is bloody open.

I'm all arms and legs as I go past. Why does my forehead begin to itch? I scratch and try to make my hand into a peaked cap hiding my face.

The stairs of course I can climb without looking. One two three . . . ten . . . indoor plant . . . turn . . . his photograph . . . neck elbow ankles like mine . . . count again . . . and there's my room.

Ma.

My hands.

The edges of my nails are black and black too are the fish-shaped fortresses in which Ma's eyes are trapped. So beautiful. So dead.

Far away. Inside the fortresses. Directionless. Whatever she says, comes travelling a long distance.

And I say—feeling what I have been feeling for years now, that it is on its way, her voice, it hasn't reached yet, possibly doesn't want to—no Ma, they're not dirty, they have always been this colour, from my childhood, and here, since you insist, let me wash them and show you.

I wash, trying to hide the black foam on my hands.

What sort of cheap soap is this, its lather is black, I grumble.

Ma laughs. *The city, not the soap*, she laughs.

This city, this present, from far away comes her laughter, *this place where you're always young. Who survives here to grow old!*

Patting me gently, she has crossed over to that other side of time. On that side there was once a city of lights. On this side, black ruins.

On that side, a son.

On this side too, a son, no . . .?

'What did you do today?' Ma asks.

'Nothing new,' I answer shortly.

'But still,' she says.

'Painting,' I say, although today there's no hobby class, no hobby class today!

'What did you paint,' Ma asks, although she knows. She's the one who packs my school bag. She's the one who checks my timetable every day. I'm lying. So that she should know, and say something. But she'll say nothing. Even if I lie.

'A purple sun,' I carry on. When the paints were at home, not with me, not with me!

'A purple sun?' Ma asks. She knows everything but will not say anything to me.

'The evening sun, a nature study,' I say, enjoying the taste of aimless lying.

'Good,' says Ma.

Aimless lying can mean something, it's not useless.

'Hey, you're laughing,' I say to her, to whom I recount all of this with much relish. All my sorrows too, with much joy, that she may listen . . .

35

This way you have of smiling quietly. All right then, I shall be quiet too.

Sometimes I do go silent, like before, amazingly, even after meeting you.

Why, I wonder. But I know. These things need a voice, their own voice, not mine. Sometimes I'm left searching for that voice.

Or is it his voice I seek? Can I find it? The voice of that story? It may seem simple, but it is not.

It should be impossible to speak when voice goes missing, but I don't hesitate to speak. Ever since you entered my life, some voice or the other has embraced my throat.

You before me. Listening. Watching. Because you arrived, I began speaking.

But did I begin to speak because you arrived? Or did you arrive because I was about to speak?

Majnu came first, Laila followed! There you go, laughing again!

Believe me, that's how it is. If you had not come I would have made you up. In milling crowds, in my stark silences I would have shut my eyes and sensed you, wherever you were. And off my voice would have wandered, towards you, to wrap you in its embrace.

Who says you can open your mouth only when there's someone sitting in front of you? Come on, whether there is someone, or there isn't, who gives a damn. Once you speak, you create a listener inside. You will sing in jungles and valleys, you will roar, and whether a passer-by stops or not, you have your listener in your soul.

After that you can never be quiet again. No, I have not gone quiet. Damn it, I will never go quiet again. I will go on speaking and you will go on listening, you will ask for more, and I will speak some more. I like you. So what's odd about that? I like you, I like you, I like you! From the beginning.

From before I even saw you. Yes, why not? Then, when I saw you, I knew it was so, just so. You are it, you're perfect. Just right.

Each time you laugh. In your own way. This is your laughter, this quiet smile.

But it's okay, I don't mind. I know you. You are kind and patient, you coax me to speak. You want me to speak.

I have not spoken till today. No one speaks in this house. In this house, speaking means switching on the machinery and letting the wheels and parts rumble.

Nothing like this has happened to you. That's why it seems strange to you. That an accidental push should have sent the people living here hurtling off a cliff, slipping and sliding, and now they're hanging precariously midway, neither able to go back nor complete the fall!

Again you laugh? Your laughter is strange sometimes. Almost like you're crying. See, your eyes are wet!

Look then, at the dry eyes of those who live in this home.

A home? Or is it just that empty space the papers are still so enamoured with? The empty space that bombs of the times leave behind, challenging time to fill it up, mingling the ones gone with the ones left behind!

Mingling is fun. Mingling with you! You know I like you. Amazing. I say absolutely anything to you. I *can* say absolutely anything to you. I have even said, I like you.

Of course, I don't know you. So what? Liking is another chemistry, quite another compound. Like your laughter.

Tell me, why do you laugh so? At nothing? I'm doing it too.

You just feel like laughing? Me too.

I just feel like liking you. And that's what I'm doing.

36

It could look like I'm rambling. The waiting, the bomb, the pieces, the silence.

Shall I apologize? No problem. I have no arrogant hang-ups about saying sorry. So here. Sorry.

But what can I do? When nothing remains in one's control. Perhaps it's different in different times. The waiting, the silence, all in fine shards like diamond dust. The fields, sky, water, too, all in pieces. The wind too, perhaps. This bit belongs to us, and that other bit, pouring out of the furnace, expels its carbon and soot across the ocean.

Send it to the people who live botched up in their story. Their eyes focused one way, hands reaching out in another, their ears and feet and ankles crowded into their horns.

There's a country in the eastern horizon of this world, with an old custom that continues till today, of bearing aloft in procession on some festival days, in a palanquin, the spirit of their deity, to reinstall it after uprooting it from its shrine. For some reason they don't call it a palanquin, they call it a *mikoshi*.

Just as we don't call the sarkari box a coffin!

This is what happens in that land—many hands hold the mikoshi up on their shoulders but what's funny is that they all face different directions. One looks back, another to one side, one faces this way, another that. And yet they walk together. United, mingled. The holy spirit in their midst.

You know, don't you, my girl, that we have our own secret mikoshi. Its name is . . .

Damn! I am sick and tired. I want to steer clear of names, of identities. *Ai dekhne waalon mujhe tak tak ke na dekho! Oh world, don't stare so strangely at me.* As if you seek around me someone else who should have been in my place.

Tumko ko bhi zamana kahin mujhsa na bana de! Some day my fate might befall you.

Of course I'm tired of this, why shouldn't I be? I wish things could be taken for what they really are. Let a cow be a cow, not a mother-in-disguise. The deception extends to everything. A plain and simple metal trunk dons a frilled cover in someone's living room and plays at being a divan transported from some royal province. Dogs feed on palak-paneer and begin to believe their front paws are human hands. As if that's not enough, when they bark, their owners hear, oh no, not barking, but clear human words, you're back, how nice, bow wow!

I get utterly exhausted by all this. Who are you, what are you? You are your roots, your roots will determine your trunk, then your branches, next the fruit and the flowers, your taste and your colour, your aim and your goal.

What about the breeze and the fertilizer and the spade and the fire and the bomb, are they nothing?

No, the record is stuck at *roots*.

Roots roots roots, on and on till we reach the banyan tree. Found in many jungles of the world. This tree is all about roots. It sprouted at the time of the earth's sprouting, through its roots, and continues to spread. Through its roots. No sooner did its roots touch the earth than it spread lustily, reaching for the sky and swooping down again to embrace the soil. Another root and yet another. Just once more. One last one, and after that one more still. Is there any limit to lust?

The tale of the root is that once upon a time there was one root and then there grew roots upon roots upon roots, sprouting from the branches and tendrils, hands and soil, spreading out, engulfing, surrounding, creating more and more forests of root. The banyan knits away at its unique tapestry and will keep knitting away obsessively into newer and newer spaces.

But those who are obsessed with roots will keep on backtracking and obsessing about the prime root!

Honestly, I'm tired. Spare me these complications. Let some things happen simply, with sheer simplicity. Let me carry this story further. A story never ends. I am telling you and may stop telling you, but it does not end there. Because by then you too have entered the story and that story too will take its own course and will move on and ahead.

Like the banyan? You might ask. Could be, why not? Strange are stories and their ways!

I am telling you a very strange story. Beyond name and root and race. Don't get fixated on origins and identity, because those born of bombs and dead of bombs have other terms of reference.

I get so tired. But tired as I am, I still repeat, in sleep and in waking—what happened, did happen, an explosion right at the centre, okay okay, no getting away from it, a bomb, a *bumb*, and then all is stealth, creeping, like a thief, a criminal, and I too, hide inside it, seen, unseen, and sometimes it's me who's seen and sometimes it's someone else.

I keep trying to gather things together. But am I gathering, or being surrounded?

Gathering, or being surrounded?

Am I zeroing in or is something surrounding me, zeroing in on me?

Again an explosion . . .? The waiting.

37

I want to move to the present. I'm trying.

But this past of mine. Which keeps slipping into my present.

I try to enter into today but fear that by the time I get there, it would have become yesterday.

Let me start again.

This is what I must do, start again and again.

So let us return to the point where life had settled calmly into a long cool breath. Let mother and father go to work, let the world carry out its worldly routine, let schools and tuitions and markets and assemblies go on at their own pace. Let me grow in years.

Let us count how old. In such a way that so many years with this one equals as many years without that one.

Let's enter the cave. Let's slumber away the years in forgotten grief.

A grief that does not scream. Just flickers like a lamp. Invisible in the light of the sun. Unfurling in the dark of the night.

Sleep strips my skin bare. If ever I begin to drift into sleep as the dark gulps down my room and the world around me dies, and from far away the sound of cars and the howl of dogs recedes to a deep murmur inside the earth and I too begin to be buried in it, it emerges, the thing wearing the ants like a cloak and then again the scratch scratch begins to peel my sleeping skin and I catch my breath and I feel locked into a box and I am but motes of dust. Thread by thread the ants are unravelling me, and my heart going thud thud thud, I wake up into the deathly silent nights.

If on such nights I find Ma sitting near me, naturally she's a ghost too. Her eyes swimming in the empty space. A part of the ghostly night.

'What happened?' she smoothes the creases of darkness from my brow.

She opens the window. 'You keep out the fresh air, that's why.'

There is no sky outside my window. I look out. I let Ma's hand iron out my breaths like a road roller straightens out a road. Inhale, exhale. In regular rhythm. Measured. One bit in, one bit out.

No respite from bits! In. Out. Inside the box.

'I can smell the scent of that big white flower,' I say.

'The flower?' Ma repeats. She looks out of the window. Then at me, strangely. She's looking at me but her gaze is somewhere else. 'There's no flower here.'

There is something there. I shiver.

'But there used to be. He had brought it. Placed the pot at this very window. A white flower had bloomed. I used to water it.'

The fragrance of the flower wafts in. Sounds simmer in the depths of the earth.

Ma's words.

'The scent of that very flower? There is something in your eyes . . . something . . . the same glance . . . as in his.'

I, too, a ghost. A part of the ghostly night.

38

Ghostly ways have ghostly bulk. They are what fill out our life! The house appears to bloom, the pictures are lifelike, from foods emanate his favourite fragrances, and no one at all knows whether it is he or us, he stretching out his hand in ours.

Father emerged from his room, a bag of bones, his body punctured. Threw a longing look at the front door. A letter the postman must have slipped in under the door, lying there. He lifts it.

But no chance of it filling him up with air. It was only my report card.

He gave it a cursory glance. 'Non-performer!' he muttered under his breath. 'Doesn't want to lift a finger to help himself . . .' he went on.

Hoping perhaps that the irritation would pump air into his punctured self.

It didn't work. He turned his eyes to the pictures. That worked. Performer par excellence! Father had kept all his report cards carefully. And his tutorials, letters, books, random scraps of paper.

He is comforted, the boy in the picture is ahead in the race. He let my card slip back to the floor, and died again, returning to his study.

But the boy in the picture, he lived still. Ma came down the stairs with a packet of leftover food.

I picked up his cane and we went out into the street.

To carry on a practice he had initiated. Cows and horses were cared for and even worshipped, but what about the poor stray dogs?

The way the dogs began to laugh and fanned us vigorously with their tails, there was no doubt it was his hand stretching out mine to feed them! Animals, I cursed inwardly, separating them with the cane so that all could get an equal share. Come on, move. No, *no*—disgusting carnivores!

Ma was content. Or as content as she could be. With his stick, like him, I was rationing out the food to the dogs. I was his heir. This was his munificence. His compassion, his desire.

No one else's desires survive here. Pinned on the wall, he directed our every move. Handed me his stick to deal with the dogs but took away with him the real stick. He would lift it ever so slightly, make the smallest gesture and there—his puppets wiggle around obligingly!

39

So. In the air? In space? In the ground? When the inside is empty, where is its inside? Surely somewhere. Because when the inside is empty, this murmuring is still there. It must begin from somewhere.

The murmuration, the susurration, the rustling. Murmur, rustle-rustle. Murmurs all scattered, all over the place, but one day we find over them a question mark that says what if we were to come together?

The question becomes sharper, more impatient, and I look around confused, is something going to happen?

Am I waiting? (Or is he?) Do we know whether the separate bits will join up or the joined bits will scatter? What is it I'm hankering for? (Or he?)

I find I have taken to looking around expectantly all the time; is something happening? No, nothing. The weather is normal. Passers-by on the street, the same as usual. But has something changed somewhere? Surely.

'Ma,' I call out.

She comes. 'What?'

But I have forgotten what.

'I don't remember,' I say. Why did I forget, I think.

Ma's brought a plate of something he liked, that she had just made.

I eat it. I have begun to like what he liked. Does that make it my taste now, or is it his still?

I look towards him and in fellow feeling touch the snack to his picture. Like one does to a god, to turn food into prasad.

'Ma,' I say again. 'Look at his thighs and look at mine.'

'Tennis,' Ma says. 'Or jogging.'

'From tomorrow, I'll go jogging,' I say, and feel somehow relieved.

But the moment I am alone, I hear again the murmuration, the susurration.

Can you hear it too? I ask the picture when no one can see me hold forth to him, away from the world where I'm silent.

Can't you understand? I say arrogantly. What language do you speak, man? Or are you dumb or what? Have you glued your tongue to your palate? Need surgery?

I'm sneering, but he's silent.

Okay, okay, I touch my ears in a gesture of penitence. Don't get mad, I'll let you be. Come on, let's make up, shake hands. Our hands touch.

Then I feel a rush of kindliness. Do they bother you? Keep interfering, don't they. You want to run away? Where to? Shall I open the cage?

I lock my eyes with his, stubbornly. I am not leaving till you answer. I stand there, staring deep, diving, drowning.

Murmuring . . . mumuring . . . louder and louder, and my unease grows. Where was it coming from? From under the earth, or from inside the sea, or from behind the sky. On the surface, everything as before. What the hell was happening? What should happen? Should anything happen at all? Then let life happen, the past and present, the wait and the story . . . the story, just the story, let me be the story, let it be my story . . .

And let me not slip through the story, nor let the story slip through me, leaving me alone again, with nothing in my grasp, just fragments floating in space . . .

Ma says I fell asleep sitting in front of the picture.

Face-to-face, he and I, and around us the murmuring. Murmur murmur. Like millions of bubbles.

Or not bubbles, frequencies.

Tuned to tell us that something will happen.

The waiting has come to breaking point, something has to happen now.

40

I had dozed off, yes. Not sitting in front of him, but in fact, completely relaxed, stretched out in his bed.

Something woke me up. There was someone in my room.

I was about to sit up when I recognized Father. In the darkness, his ghostly gait.

What could I do? Lay there quietly, eyelids shut tight. Father inspecting every single thing. Touching the books. Touching the pen stand. What the hell, I wondered when I felt his hand brush against the wonder on my face, passing lightly over my lips.

That really startled me. Should I open my eyes or not, I hesitated and slowly my lashes began to lift.

What on earth was Father up to? He was walking with great care, one palm outstretched, touching the wall, stroking and caressing it on the way to the door, which he opened softly. He turned towards me before going out, I felt he met my eyes. But in the dark I could not be sure.

I let a few seconds pass and then got up soundlessly to follow, totally confounded, my god, what was happening?

He was in Ma's room now, his arm outstretched as before, feeling the wall with his fingers stretched out. Like some kind of magic ritual.

Ma kept sleeping.

The hand never left the wall, went down the stairs, then round one room after another, and around the rest of the house, the entire house! Like he was fulfilling a vow.

I keep watching quietly as in the same pose he goes into the kitchen, into his study, and all around the hall.

The spread out hand of the shadow steadily tracing the walls of the house. Like an act of worship.

Then the shadow opened the front door. Turned around a second time. This time as if to say goodbye.

I jumped. Out of fear for Ma? Or for Father? I couldn't understand what to do. Should I stop him? Can I? Oh, the weight of such decisions on my fragile shoulders!

But he was gone. Leaving the door ajar.

Flustered I raced after him, slipping on my shoes and clicking the door shut behind me.

Left or right, left, then right, ah there he was. A mere shadow. With me after it. In my jogging shoes.

Oh, we walked on like that for a long time. The shadow ahead, I following. When the shadow stopped, I did too. The shadow would turn to look at me and I would panic, what was I to say if he asked me what was going on.

But suddenly I felt the shadow was not looking at me at all. Rather it was looking past me. At the path we were leaving behind. At the house.

It was eerie.

And then the weirdest thing. We had reached the nala, the long open drain at the end of our neighbourhood. In the black of the night it looked quite lovely. On its side grew a plant with that scented flower. Just one flower in a pot. White in colour.

Father reached out and plucked it. Plucked it and brought it to his nose, inhaling dramatically as if it was his last breath of oxygen, and then he tucked the flower behind his ear.

After this when he turned to walk on, it was clear from his suddenly decisive gait that it was finished, the desire to turn back.

I was in such a state that I wasn't even afraid. I just kept watching and watching.

The shadow moving ahead. Further and further away from me.

For a long time I trailed behind at an even pace, never once letting the flower out of sight. That white flower tucked behind the ear.

The shadow kept moving alongside the water. Faster now. I'm jogging to keep up, panting. It would have made Father boast, *look at the difference between the younger generation and us.*

The water was full of stars.

Before I knew it, the shadow had bent, its cupped palm carrying water from the nala to its mouth and when it straightened up I knew this was the water that made you forget. The world and its business and its tongues and all its fetters—all had been forgotten now.

Smell the flower and desire dies, drink the water and forgetting overtakes memory.

The ceremony was complete.

What was I going to tell Ma, I began to tremble and felt so drained that I didn't notice the shadow vanish and didn't remember how and when my broken heart took me back home and threw me on my bed.

41

'Let me be . . .'

Half asleep you realize it's you speaking. Meaning me. Ma was shaking my shoulders to wake me up. She stopped on hearing my voice. 'Come on, get up and go,' she says. She means, 'Go jogging.'

'Not me,' I say, slowly descending from the peaks of sleep, 'Him.' But the moment I say 'him,' I fall to the bottom in one swoop and my eyes snap open.

It's not true that sleep is senseless. Just as I say 'him,' I am filled with the knowledge of sleep. I realize it wasn't Father touching those walls. Stunned, I turn to look at the picture.

'Happy birthday,' Ma says and kisses me.

'But your shoes?' she rushes after me with my jogging shoes as I tear down the stairs, barefoot.

'I've already done my jogging,' I fling back at her and sliding past Father, I jerk open the front door.

Right in front of me, on the doorstep, that plant, of the scented white flower.

'When did you bring this?' I turn to Ma who had hurried after me. I mean from the edge of the nala. When?

'I got it for your birthday,' says Ma, in all innocence. As if I don't understand for whose birthday it is.

But Ma doesn't understand that he has already inhaled the fragrance of the flower, the flower that brought freedom from desire.

'The flower?' I ask.

'Son, it blossoms in the rains,' says Ma, looking pleased with my interest in the plant.

Do you know what I did then? I shut up.

And thus on my eighteenth and his thirty-something birthday, early in the morning, all of a sudden I fall silent. I return to my room and lying quietly on the bed, looking at him—or his picture—I think about what had happened in the night.

For some reason I am overwhelmed by a feeling of gratitude towards him. He, who has given me such company that I have never been alone.

Oh well, the date is yours after all, my friend. Or would have been.

I hold out my hand. As usual. Happy birthday.

Then I pull it back, sadly. What fun it might have been to really—really—shake hands with you.

I look down at my hands. Not bad. Not as strong as yours but not spindly either. There's something about us, you and me, something similar. Husbands and wives begin to look like each other after years of living together. Even cats and dogs begin to look a bit like their owners after a while. And we have been together a long while, haven't we? I have been surrounded by you. You the model, I the clay. The very flow of blood through my flesh has been moulding me in your shape.

Today I want him there. I want to make him happy. I want to comfort him for the life that has given him such a nasty jolt. What fun we would have had, forget all this business about soul and god, I would have said, ours is the age to chase girls, so come on!

I want to tell him fondly, listen, your Ma is wonderful, and your Father . . . well, what can I say about him . . . but you don't mind, do you?

The picture stares at me like a picture. Dead and framed. He has heard nothing.

But I have heard. The commotion in front of the buildings on the street outside. Toothpaste foaming in my mouth, I open the window.

Workers on cranes, high up in the sky, tying sparkling lengths of cloth that would flutter like colourful dupattas. The workers on the crane and the dupattas tied to the stars, cheeky, flying free, try and stop us.

So here it's our birthday, but there it's also a festival the world celebrates. Star-shaped lanterns and shimmering candles outside homes and shops. At street corners and in the lanes, and in courtyards and backyards, big triangular trees stand ready, wrapped in cellophane. They wait quietly to be let out, when they will glitter with lights and dolls and streamers.

42

Now listen, when you open the window you haven't touched for ages and see there in front of you, workers swinging merrily in the air and banners waving colourfully about them, the stirrings return, that *kulbul kulbul* inside begins to grow, to mischievously blow sadness into iridescent bubbles. Kulbul kulbul, the silence lifts. The bubbles are floating in the air, reflecting the colours of the banners. I stand at the window.

'Happy birthday,' Ma is by my side. She pops a sweet in my mouth and kisses my forehead. 'Happy birthday, my child.'

Mother's blessings in which truth and lie are indistinguishable. Today you are eighteen.

Today you are older . . .

Eighteen is what you are today. Today once more you are eighteen . . . May all your dreams come true.

Oh, may all your dreams come true! Live a long life, thrive, blossom . . . May my years be added to your life . . . Today you have crossed thirty . . .

No, today you are eighteen again!

Her screams so silent, where do they go? On her tangled branches I rest my head.

This was our annual ritual, of the two of us—or of us three. Now I will lie down.

I lie down directly under his picture. He bending over me like a god or a demon.

My eyes close and Ma's hands bless me, caressing me gently. Caress me, spreading out the blessings. Caressing me, she spreads out my body. Like my body is the skin of her son and he can enter it and wear me like a coat or a trouser. Never will the red ants scratch again, nor red rashes bloom. Softly, methodically, she puts his head in mine, his arms in my arms and his legs in my legs.

Sweet agony where his hands tear their way out of my arms, his feet push through my legs.

His extra fifteen years have to stuff themselves into my slighter frame!

Both of us—all three of us—are silent. But I can't tell Ma that he really *is* silent, the picture has died, it's just an empty frame hanging up there now.

That this too is a ritual: to trace the walls and smell the white flower and sip the water of forgetfulness and transcend to another world. The flower that ends desire, the water that ends memory.

I can't tell Ma that her language is now unknown to him, he no longer understands what she says.

Ma looks overwhelmed with gratitude that I have resurrected him so! She sees us both, eighteen years old, lying one inside the other, stretched out on the floor on that glorious day.

In the innocent expectation of eighteen years, lightly, so lightly, the tremulous rhythm like a bird in my heart, eager to spread its wings, to keep spreading and spreading them.

Ready to take a leap out of the window, and who gives a damn if one flies or falls!

43

To turn eighteen and for the bubbles to go kulbul kulbul. Where do these bubbles bubble up from? Kulbul kulbul.

From the scattered pieces. From longings buried deep and dark, joining up in stealth, searching out their missing halves and quarters, hoping—still—to become whole? A story. A human. An eighteen-year-old . . .?

Today I'm eighteen. Inexplicable joy bubbling in my heart. I don't know how long this has been going on, this joyous bubbling. Preparations for the party downstairs and here I am in this strange state. Must be because I have turned eighteen. We are eighteen.

Oh to be eighteen!

Everyone waits to be eighteen. Whoever can manage it, turns eighteen at least once. This has nothing to do with bombs. Even if there's a bomb you must turn eighteen. So that all the likes, dislikes, good, evil, floating in the air, just once, simply and innocently, may enter the skin.

The sweet little bird of youth flutters in my heart as I walk down the stairs. The usual guests have arrived. His pictures are up, the flowers he loved, water trickling over from the flower vases, his favourite dishes displayed on the table, his memory on every face, no one crying, no one laughing, the world outside too, getting all spruced up for festivities, merry singing, happy birthday to you, Ma looking at me like she can see his presence in me, Father looking at me like he can see his absence in me, am I present or absent, *happy birthday to you and you are dead too*, and I am in a new shirt and my forehead is itching, the watch on my wrist is his, but it's fantastic, with a calculator and the time around the world, there are candles on the cake, the flame is restive, aware it is about to be blown out, my hands are at a loss about what to do, should they be in my pocket, his friends are chattering away, shall I put my hands behind me, the walls stand upright, I am shy, I am tense, the floor lies flat, the air I breathe is restless, sure it's about to be blown to bits, the house lies prostrate, shall I lie down or no, keep standing, shouldn't I smile, I am smiling, they are singing *happy birthday to you*, why am I smiling, people are singing, I'm singing too, *happy birthday to you*, why am I singing happy birthday to you on my own birthday!

I flounder.

They all stop singing. I turn red.

Then I laugh.

They all burst out laughing.

Not Father. Ma smiles softly. The guests get into the mood—tap their feet, drink and eat. Now *this* is a party, a birthday party. An eighteenth-birthday party.

Really, who knows where the bubbles come from? They send out iridescent filaments that wind themselves round my heart.

Since when, you ask? I ask too. I don't know. Maybe they were waiting for the hero to turn eighteen.

Eighteen.

In the powerful language of the world it is called *eighteen*, in other languages, *attharah*, *pathinettu*, *chogye.* At eighteen you can vote, you can drink, you can choose which parent to be with, you can decide to be on your own, you can rightfully ask for your explode, or be exploded by a bomb.

Goodness, he is eighteen today, wow you are eighteen today, oh my you are eighteen again, what does he want to do, what do you want to do, what, what do you want to do?

The questions kept coming, and I said, *I want to go and study in that well-known university*, and tried to balance on my spoon some morsel I had picked up to eat.

44

The very air froze in amazement. Believe me. I'm not exaggerating.

Suddenly.

I mean suddenly, without warning. It grew sort of darkish in the room. And at the precise moment someone pressed a switch, the electricity went off. As if the switch had been pressed to turn off the light, rather than to turn it on!

Absolute stillness. As at an announcement, quiet please, switch off your mobiles, the curtain is about to rise, the drama about to begin.

I stood flabbergasted at my own words. A plate in my hand and food balancing on a spoon, ready to fall.

I was stunned of course. But perhaps the others too. Who was on stage, who off it? Who on this side, who on the other side, of the curtain?

The darkness so intense, the picture had become invisible. The lights have gone, I thought.

And back they came. As if the curtain had gone up.

There I am, there's the plate, the spoon, I'm stunned, and of course it was me on the stage and the audience waiting with bated breath, what was he going to say?

Once on stage, once the curtain rises, even the most bewildered actor is energized, fills with air. The spotlight turns on you and fear vanishes. Once the audience is in darkness, it's me in the light, me and my role. Even statues would come alive.

'Yes, why not,' I gave the jammed air a shake, 'I want to study there.'

What's that, I asked my ears and thinking it was something from outside, I opened the door. The darkness flowed in like a breeze. Gently. Then faster and faster. Carrying with it an echoing hum that all could hear. A humming, an echoing.

Where was it coming from, that humming? Not humming exactly, because it had no tune. No scaling up and down of notes. A single note strangled in one place, echoing in a monotone. A disturbing rasping sound. A crying. Almost like crying.

In Ma's throat! Not outside. Like a live wire dangling in the breeze and vibrating with a thin electric screech.

The sound from her throat, toneless, tuneless, spread around me and wavered around the guests. Not loud but unmistakable.

Ma is crying.

Suddenly my heart leapt. A jolt of electricity went round the room.

A tune circled the room, round and round, hypnotically. *Ma is crying! It's a party today! Happy birthday to you! But you are dead too!* Round and round and round. Ma is crying and the door is open.

The darkness flows in like air, flows faster and faster, in a frenzy, faster, faster, and darkness dissolves in more darkness.

But wait, no, this is something else, these are the hundreds of transparent plastic bags that had held the triangular trees, for the festival.

Who was it who had turned on the air to flow so fierce, fattening the empty bags, turning them into live things billowing before our house? Who was it—surely someone—had propelled these bags towards our front door, to dance their wanton dance?

In the darkness, flailing about in the wind beneath the banners glittering against the sky, the bags flap and bounce in obscene abandon. The blustery wind pulls them up, flings them down, up, down. Like obese flapping birds, they fill the air.

Ma kept crying.

45

Ma had not cried in fifteen years.

No one knew what to do. Silent. Waiting.

That was a mistake. Staying silent. Waiting. If only they hadn't, if only they had carried on drinking sherbet and things, munching snacks, carried on adjusting the buckles of their belts or pulling out tissue from their handbags, they could have ignored and wiped out with cunning indifference, the words that had escaped so thoughtlessly from my mouth and how comfortably everything would have slid back under the familiar cover of gloom and melancholy. That curtain of calm, which for fifteen years had covered the one broken by the bomb, while in front of it were the ones joined by the bomb, that one-big-family with his loving gaze on us, blessing us from his pictures.

The picture was silent too, and everyone waiting. For me to say something, do something. To be their saviour. To explain, to deny, to comfort.

No one wants to remember what my words were exactly, nor by asking, to bring their meaning alive once again. So they were silent.

Which was a mistake.

If someone waits for you to speak and you stay silent, you're the stronger person. Your arms seem to lift slightly from your sides and the other is convinced that it's not air that fills them but the power of growing muscle.

That was a mistake, they stayed silent and my words could not now be forgotten. What I said sank deep, imprinted into my mind. Permanent, indelible letters that smouldered inside me. That could burst into flames at any time.

I turned.

Outside the open door the blustery birds were at their crazy dance. Leaping up and down. In Ma's throat the buzzing of a trapped bee.

If you haven't cried in fifteen years, and then after fifteen years you cry, your crying becomes a bumblebee trapped in your throat.

'Ma,' I said.

Ma broke into wild sobbing.

If you don't cry in fifteen years and then after fifteen years you cry, this is the only way you can possibly cry. As if this is all you can do now. In roaring sobs. Her nose swollen. Her eyes spat out by the fish. Hiccups racking her body. Her face flowing with tears. The wind, tangled in a curtain, reached out and touched her. Thinking it was my hand, Ma jerked it off. The curtain slumped.

'Ma, be strong,' I said. She became quiet.

Suddenly. Very quiet.

For a long never-ending moment her eyes pierced me like spears. Cold. Black. Glittering.

'Strength, I have,' she said. 'Him, I don't.'

Him. His name. Ma mentioned his name for the first time. After fifteen years, in public.

Everyone's eyes turned automatically to the picture. He was smiling and the dark was dancing in his eyes. Dark waves in the darkness.

I had made Ma cry. It was he who quietened her down. The buzzing bee now entered my throat.

How well I know that moment in which you die and you come alive. In the same moment the meeting and in it, the parting.

'He,' I took his name. For the first time in fifteen years, in front of them all. 'He is gone.'

Her imperious eyes rested on me briefly. Like a queen she turned away, head held high, shoulders straight, and she walked up the stairs. Where the mind is without fear and the head is held high . . .!

Suddenly I felt a slap land hard on my cheek. The morsel I was about to put into my mouth bounced off my plate and fell to a pulp on the floor.

'That was a killer blow!' Father burst out, as he went up the stairs after Ma.

What did he mean, that I had dealt a killer blow to Ma, or to him, my dead friend, or did he mean his killer blow to me?

That was some blow he had landed on my cheek!

46

I ask myself why I answered that question the way I did. There could have been so many answers.

That's where I want to go. Which I did say.

I want to go somewhere else. Which I did not say. Or *I don't know*.

Or *nowhere*.

Or said nothing. Heard nothing. Deaf, dumb.

But what I said, I said, and it was done. *The horse had bolted from the stable, the birds had picked the field clean*, whatever. It was too late now.

Was it at his signal that I spoke? Did he smile his instructions from the picture? Did he make me see his prospectus from that university in Father's room?

But the flower and the water?

Did I say it to please Ma and Father, *look, I am so like him? Let us remember him together, make his name come alive?* Or did I say it just to tease them? Boo!

Or did I say it out of guilt that I am here, and he is not? Paying a sort of fine. For surviving? For being flung aside safely?

Or so as not to be flung aside any more? To refuse to be flung aside?

Was I trying to be a hero? Did I mean to be loving? Or to assert my right? By mistake? Obstinately? In defiance? Craving recognition? For the sake of those roots? On behalf of those pieces? Why did I say what I did?

Unreasoningly, purposelessly?

Because reason and purpose are the mafias of the world, they grab you and tell you, go fly those planes like bulldozers, and go smoke out those beards like rats from their caves. Go to America . . . go to Afghanistan . . .

Or perhaps I just said what I did because the game of hide and seek was over now, I had turned eighteen, that special moment at which every question spread its wings.

At eighteen, even the empty space dreams of becoming a flying saucer and says *go fly away, nothing holds you back, you're not buried anywhere, you belong nowhere, you're fortunate, you have no limits!*

It's nonsense to say you're fortunate if you know your mother, your father, your jungle. What would have been your great achievement then? Had your mother been a Jew, off you'd go to Israel to write reams about it; if your father was Mizo, you would lose yourself in Mizoram. That's it, right? But imagine if all you had was the empty space. Then the whole world is yours to interpret.

I tell you this age belongs not to the one who belongs somewhere, but to the one who belongs nowhere.

For what does a blast do? It just shreds you and scatters you. Shreds of fire, water, earth, air, sky. Nothing looks like itself any longer. Turns into something else. Anything else. An idli, a finger.

So shall we conclude then that on one side stood Ma, her crying, Father, his slap, my dead friend, his smile, town after town on fire, and on the other side, an empty space?

Yes, that's what we should conclude, I think.

And we should also conclude that I'm eighteen, my arms fill with life, pick up the empty space with a flourish and swing it round and round like an empty sack and oh, what can't I fill it with, and with a powerful sweep I'll let it land, where should I let it land so that it may explode and my desire can burst out of it—love, I'm in love!

47

The sun rose like it had turned eighteen too. With a new sort of glow.

In the darkness Ma was watching my face—or his, what difference does it make—watching me pull on a T-shirt, lace up my jogging shoes. Watching me go carefully down the stairs but she knows I'm bounding down. I walked out of the door but she knows I've leapt out of the window.

Her worried face just behind the door. My jogging shoes just outside. The first morning of youth. It makes your heart long to run. Run, and the world runs with you. Run, and you light up the morning with your speed.

That special time of the morning. When the light is not yet light, but the dark is no longer dark. The day is about to begin, and in its anticipation light bulbs are coming on, people waking, getting ready, preparing to go to work. Windows gleam softly like lanterns. Their glass panes envelope themselves in their own warm light. The concrete buildings like hills and valleys in the ruddy glow. On their surfaces flicker the secrets and lives lived inside. Someone sweeps, others hang out clothes, unfold newspapers, some not quite awake, the air is full of romance. I run, the morning twinkles. There's water in the gutter. Not a gutter, but a stream. My shoes are brand new. From them rise a purple hue. They light up the sky and wind and water. They splash the purple all over the morning, my shoes!

I stop under that tree where I will meet you one day. I would pause to catch my breath under its swaying branches and you'd ask me the way.

But not today. Today I will stop under it all unknowing, admiring its foliage in my colourless neighbourhood.

I will run and run, circling the neighbourhood, inhaling the fresh breath of the morning. It was the moment of creation.

I run and run in the purple dawn, a spring in my steps. Like I don't know if I have feet or wings, and how many, and how to settle into a rhythm! Like I don't know what I am, and I don't care! A tiny little ant that leaps like a frog, that becomes a blackbuck tearing along, and now it's a bull lowering its horns threateningly, and then a lovely butterfly absorbed in its own flight, that settles on and becomes the flower dancing gracefully with the bee and in school we are taught this is how a bee buzzes, but those illiterates didn't know that *this* is the song of being eighteen; no bee, no flower, no butterfly or bull, blackbuck or toad or ant could manage this!

He must have felt like this too, he who was taken hostage by the reason-and-purpose mafia and killed and thrown down before his parents. I remembered him that morning, as I went running at dawn.

Feeling him running along like me, how he would have started to pant, to become drenched in sweat, bending his head to sniff his armpits, inhaling his own heady smell, running and running, amidst the waking engines of cars and buses, past the bustle of people starting their day.

Are they staring at me? But I don't cringe, not today.

Nor would he have. And why should he, what for? Would they ever think, looking at him, this is him, he is the one? The bomb guy. Silenced by the fear of the bomb.

Never! He never was the bomb guy. He was about to become it. But he never got to know.

But even if he knew he wouldn't have been scared. He wouldn't even have been scared of the bomb. He would have run ahead to where it lay quiet and bounced it about like a ball.

His pace wouldn't have changed even in front of the house. Mine didn't, either. But he would have dumped the ball in some bush. I didn't have a ball or else I too . . .

So without hiding anything in a bush, hiding only my inner speed behind my careful outer gait, I came towards the door. I asked him silently, if you returned home after all these years, how would you feel?

48

This is the door, I thought he would have thought.

I stopped there, let me think for a moment or two.

This door. The door of my home. Where I was born and grew up. Along the sides, the fragrant flowering plants that would shed their blooms below the trees and which Ma would gather to float in clay saucers of water.

But hey, no plants, no flowers, no clay saucers?

Has something changed? Yes, something has changed.

I look around, what's this, garbage everywhere? Paint peeling off the walls, plaster flaking, rust running up the pipes like a skin disease.

Such sadness. I would never even have known the place if . . .

if . . . those old shops hadn't still been there.

And these new shops? This multi-storey mall? These hadn't been there. Sorrow rises too, like the new buildings. There had been just empty space here, all the way to the sky. Father used to say we must put in a complaint, people keep filling it with rubbish.

Father! Suddenly the heart stopped still. He used to say there would be a park there. With swings. I'd look out of my window and throw a tantrum, 'I want to go there right now, now. Now.' Eyes turn upwards. My window. Why is it shut though? I never ever closed the window, even if it made me cuddle inside a quilt. Who lives in my room? Where has he come from, to spoil its style?

I don't know, I thought. I, not he! Feeling a trifle nervous. Wonder if he would have liked me? Who are you and where have you come from? What should I say? What do I know? In fact, I don't know! And why open the window when there is no sky left? For me the window is a wall, and on this side of it I live, in your room, in your life. Ma though, whenever she can, slyly opens the window.

Ma! He staggers. The brief word surged like the sea. I placed my hand on the door and gently touched her forehead, cheeks, nose. Ma's face. In all these years only one thought had lived inside her, where would I be, in what condition, when would I return?

I touch my forehead to the door. I am on this side, and Ma on the other.

How could she know I am here? If she did, why would she be smoking cigarette after cigarette, smoking herself away? Yes, that's what she would be doing, waiting for me.

Why Ma, why do you waste yourself away? Relax, I'm here, look, safe. In one piece! Taller? I'm not sure. How much taller can one grow after eighteen? But perhaps a little fatter. I have to admit I was not starving or else how would I be here! Not your cooking of course, and not my favourite goodies but I was fine, I am fine, absolutely okay, not starving or thirsty, abandoned somewhere. Thanks to your blessings. Ah, yes, I look a bit darker, don't I? No, no, I did not get burnt, only by the sun! It's a healthy tan. I am darker than you but that's fine—shouldn't sons be a shade or two darker than their mothers?

Ma, I opened the door.

Couldn't see anyone inside. No sound. The same old table with its glass top, the ceramic water jug too. The same old wooden tray, whose corner I had broken. Right there, where it had always been. I bent over it and examined the crack.

Have you people changed nothing at all? The same decor? The same curtains, furniture, still carrying on them the wounds of my rowdiness? Surely you could have changed what was damaged?

Everything the same, like I had never left? Even the flowers I liked.

But now I don't like these any more. I have changed. Years have been added to me. Shall I shout: change them, their colour is fake? See, the stems are encased in tubes injected with fake colour. Loud, synthetic, garish. Like poison up their stalks. Like mummified corpses.

All this must change, I feel an obstinacy grow. After all these years, you must realize I have become someone else. I am no longer that person. Now I like white flowers. I don't look like I used to, see.

Photographs everywhere. I look nothing like them.

I'm standing near a picture. That's his forehead, this mine, that's his nose, here's mine, this is his wrist and look, this is mine.

Filled with memorabilia, full of silence, a perfect pyramid. A slight movement.

Ma.

I'm back, I am about to say. My finger on the photograph.

Ma sees, and says, 'I know it now. He will never return.'

49

We began the preparations.

As simply as she would hand him a cup of tea, Ma took the box and gave it to Father—*here*.

What a tiny little box. I'm big and I'm stunned.

Where was the huge coffin I recalled seeing in my childhood? This was more like Ma's jewellery box. Velvet inside and on it, a diamond stud!

It's me who's big now, he's so tiny.

But it's not as if the bomb had become a mere pellet. It remained a bomb and all that had remained unsaid so far, was being said with the rituals.

I emptied out the hall, furniture was lifted, shifted, into Father's room and outside. Father blundering around, touching this and that, standing to the side, watching the preparations for the final rites.

It didn't seem right to have him witness his own funeral rites, and that too in all kinds of *filmi* poses, rakishly looking down from his photographs. All over the place in fancy frames.

So all his pictures were taken off the walls, and just one simple picture remained, not big or small, not leader or sportsman, nothing special about it, and Ma asked me to place it beside the box.

Once more, the box went onstage. One last time.

A sad day. Many people started crying. Today, the child will breathe his last, they knew this. What had not been allowed to happen so far was about to happen today.

Once again Ma Father the box and I. The box Ma I and Father. I Ma the box and Father.

And whatever else remained in the world, present there on that day of grieving.

And whatever rites and rituals remained, present too, in that grieving.

Like there was an ocean that had retreated—or so you arrogantly thought—at your disdain of it. You stared at it contemptuously, and it retreated further. Further and further it retreated, and over so many years, all that remained in its place was dry sand. You thought you had chased the ocean away? You think you're different—while others bow to the waves, you would play with the sands! But listen all of you, arguing against religion and rituals, you never understood, this ocean was a seasoned player! It was never scared, it never retreated. It took on your challenge and was preparing to strike. What you thought was its retreat was its wily move to gather strength and hit back with double, triple force. It ducked, slipped back a couple of steps, gathered all its fury and now, when it lashes out, you'll be flung to the ground and dripping wet, soaked through and through.

One after the other they came, the rites and rituals, like overpowering waves. High, strong, wild with mourning, to flood this dry, parched place and to carry it off with them.

There were flowers and prayers and water and fire. Sacred words and religious books. Grief wore a watch on its wrist. Children waited for the prasad of Pepsi. The empty house filled with the fumes of incense. Burning one's eyes, making noses run.

So much smoke for the second time in his life. Ma took him into her lap lovingly. Father blessed him, face flushed. In the familiar reek of fire and smoke I too remembered him: how must you be feeling, leaving us all and going away, you do want to leave us now, don't you? You *are* leaving us now, aren't you?

This was his last rite, the last nail in his coffin.

Only then will he be able to die, blown to pieces as he was, poor thing, dragged and pulled this way and that, whom we stretched into a gnarled old tree with its loose bark hanging, to sit upon its branches to grow old ourselves, waiting for the branches to crumble, and to settle our accounts for good!

50

Oh, you're crying! Tears flowing endlessly. My heart blooms with joy.

This is how a story should be heard. Like it has transported you inside itself. Into that whirlpool of sorrow. Like me. *With* me? My princess!

Exactly like you, that's how a princess should be. A soft glow on the face, eyebrows arched to the sky, and all your senses coming alive with the story so that it seems you aren't listening to it from outside, but have slipped right into the middle of it.

Listen to another saying of the ancients—it's not the story that goes wrong, but the one reading it. If the reader is gifted, even what's unfinished, what's merely hinted at, uncurl their possibilities. Because such readers don't treat the story like a toke of grass to drug that proud creature called the brain.

Oh no, skilful readers fearlessly offer all their senses to the story. Don't care if it drowns them, or sets them afloat or lashes at them like a snake bite. *Jab pyar kiya to darna kya!* Fear, and in love?

So you're my princess, and princess of the story too, no one else can be. Like it's done these days, I'll give you the post first, and afterwards advertise it! Only one with brows like this, and who listens like this to a story, as if she is making it up herself, only she may apply!

Shall I make it all legal this way? For people want it legal these days, it's all about legal and illegal; moral or immoral doesn't matter!

Look at the way bombs too, one way or another, become legal. Like it's decided, here, in this region, some country could have nuclear ambitions, so before anything actually happens, come on, completely legally, let's take our own bombs there. Pre-emptive action!

The problem is that whatever story you tell these days, at some point in it, at some crossing or junction, a bomb is likely to pop up. It's up to you if that makes you want to call all stories bomb stories, or not.

It does mean though that if everything includes talk of the bomb, the opposite is also true, that everything else carries on inside the bomb. Like in this story of mine there's this, there's that, there's love, there's you! The bomb will reappear, again and again, from inside, from outside, from near and far, destroying all borders and divides, it will come united in diversity and diverse in unity, didn't I say, it will come again and again and then again! And with it will come all those other thrills and the story will move along.

Where will it go? Don't ask yet. Just now here you are, listening, slipping into the story yourself. Here I am, telling the story, admiring you listening, so enraptured by you that I myself step out of the tale. Moving towards each other, midstream, you and I. And on the other bank I stand, watching both of us—watching myself speak, watching you listen. Drawn to one, and to the other! Enamoured of you and a little bit, because of your tenderness, enamoured of myself!

And now what happens next? Who knows? With a good storyteller and a good story, my mysterious enchantress, you never know what's coming. Because something doesn't become a story if you just stumble across it, pick it up and hand it over unchanged. Life and its image, exactly alike. Boring, predictable, *that's* no story.

A good story is one which when reflected in the mirror looks like something else. At the very least, Adam and Eve must become Edam and Ave!

But why apply the minimum condition of 'at least' to a story? The story must run free and bold, in itself, in my telling and in your listening. We will weave it as we go along together, fascinated sometimes by it and sometimes by ourselves. You and me and it and damn the rest of the world!

Right, so what was I saying?

That I cried and I made you cry, but also that I was eighteen and the hero of the story, and even in those days of sadness there was a spring in my step—I would land ever so lightly, the merest bounce, and I had wings, not feet, made for the skies, not earth.

51

What's the big deal about crying. Even if there's a spring in your step, you could feel like crying. Up goes the bier, and riding on it, a tiny jewellery box, and your heart breaks.

I smooth out the creases in Ma's clothes, she cries. She looks towards me to give me some instruction, and she cries. She just keeps crying, slowly and steadily.

Father's eyes are bloodshot.

The rites are over and people are sobbing the way they do at a *bidai*, when the daughter's palanquin is lifted for departure after her marriage. The last farewell, this house is no longer yours.

The bier is lifted on to the shoulders of aged Father and youthful me. Father weeps, he should be where that box is, that was rightfully his place and the son's damned shoulder should have been here, not there . . . Ma weeps, for her son was not inside any more, nor outside. And I cry inconsolably, how small he had become, smaller than me, smaller than a little boy, my baby brother, he had been shrunk into this and no one could do a thing.

Okay, so here's what happened, believe it or not. Dark clouds gathered in the sky, nothing unusual about that. Nor about the fact that it began to rain. But to rain precisely at that moment, just as we set out, that wild uncontrolled downpour?

We started walking. The town deluged in rain.

And in the middle of it all, the bier getting soaked. Lines of umbrellas along the sides.

Oh god, he's getting wet, Father sobs.

I hold an umbrella over my brother.

This is how the box-procession proceeded.

But not to a graveyard or a crematorium or to a riverbank. Not to an association of a caste society, or to an all-faith meeting place or to a temple or a mosque. Instead it went to the gate of an educational institution.

Until then the city of umbrellas had followed behind, but now it flowed into the grounds and covered it in black.

Mournful music played and we, his small family, alone, so lonely, walked on. Towards the marble memorial engraved with his name and achievements, waiting with open arms to receive him.

This time, flowers wouldn't entomb him, but stone.

That moment—oh, don't cry, don't, or I will too—that moment in which Father turned the diamond stud towards Ma and she kissed it and I touched it with a finger and then placed my hand on her shoulder, and suddenly the sun slid out from between the clouds like a child slipping down a slide.

The sudden snapping shut of umbrellas like a salute. I see the memorial, bright and shining.

Nothing remained to be done there. We came away.

52

This is the illusion. The day gets over and you think it has ended. But the day keeps on coming. I mean, look at the insightfulness of Hindi-walas, they have the same word *kal* for the day gone by and for the day to come! Kal is over but kal is always yet to come!

That is why the sensible thing is not to remember. For if you remember you will keep remembering.

But how could I make Ma understand? No one could.

She cries and cries. Until dawn. By my bedside.

Ma. I sit up. Why are you crying? Useless question.

I lay her down. Start stroking her back. She keeps crying. Don't cry, Ma, I say, pulling the covers up her body.

I miss him. She says, sobbing. Shhh. Shhh.

I keep remembering him, she says. It will pass. I console her.

It doesn't go. I can't stop remembering him. She cries and cries.

It will be okay, Ma, everything will be all right, I keep patting her. Keep patting her because I'm afraid to stop.

The moment I stop, she says, let's go.

It was early in the morning when we stepped out. The flower sellers were spreading out their flowers. We chose large white flowers and made our way to his memorial.

The large maidan and far away, in the corner, him. The sage of the dawn, the sun, bestowing his rays from above. Looking down on us as we cross the maidan. Ma has a lamp in her hand, I hold the flowers. Ma's shawl flapping and flickering as we cross the field. She would light the lamp at the memorial, I would place the flowers near it.

Now we will turn around. Move further and further away from the memorial. Only the flame of the lamp and Ma's shawl will keep flickering together.

When there is no one there, and Ma has left, where will the flickering go?

Father had come out of his room when we returned home. I don't know if he knew where we had been. He wasn't going to break his silence with me suddenly and ask.

Whether he bothered to ask Ma where she had gone and why she hadn't taken him, I don't know that either. After that whenever Ma wanted it, she and I would go together, she would light the lamp and I would change the flowers.

But right then, he at his door, I with Ma laying out breakfast on the table. Rinsing out cups and plates and fruit.

He just stood there.

I turned. Turned towards him fully. Looked him in the eye. He was shivering slightly, with a fever.

'Go,' I said, 'Put on a sweater. Ma's making tea.'

53

It would seem natural to catch a fever if you're old and get drenched in the rain.

But there's something else here, though you may not agree. Like a sty in one's eye, once it appears, will come again a full seven times and if you taste blood once you will become a blood-sucker, and if it's night, you become darkness and if eighteen is upon you, you become unvanquishable, your teeth are sharp, your nails slash deep like a knife and with one blow you can fell whoever you want, that's the kind of strength you have! Newly come upon you!

In one stroke they became completely dependent on me. It was like he'd been struck down. *I'm in your hands now, do what you will, care for my wounds, or conduct my last rites.*

Aah, you glare at me, at my braggart tone, but really, it was I, not the rain, that gave Father fever. I needed that fever, or else, this Father of mine, would he have allowed me to take charge?

Medicine at this time and soup at that, and give him a set of clothes if he wants to change, Ma would instruct before stepping out. Me, alone in the house, with my ill father.

At first I didn't really get what had happened. Then I began to get alarmed. That paralysed me. But finally I began to smile. And that freed me. I began to do what was necessary. But also much more.

Sponging him thoroughly. Wringing the towel in hot water. Rubbing away diligently. On his back, behind the ears, between the fingers, into the furrows on his skin, over the prominent, skeletal bones. Father so weak that he could say neither yes or no. I full of energy, sprucing him up like smart youths lovingly polish their motorbikes and scooters. The handle, the seat, the mudguard, number plate, the accelerator!

Where is your Ma, Father wanted to ask, but could only weakly groan and give up. Not *my* mother, but *his*, the thought must have risen afresh. This poor helpless, bedridden emperor, powerless to do a thing!

Open your mouth, and I would shove the thermometer in like

I was taping shut a babbling mouth.

He was raging with fever. I checked the temperature again. Really very high. It scared me. If something went wrong, Ma would never forgive me, but he would have even more reason to curse me. That his body burnt with fever because of me!

His glance was accusing anyway. As he looked at the medicines.

He is not able to meet my eye.

I don't say a thing, just point at the medicines, and he swallows them.

When the body becomes so weak, the mind can't even play at being a toy tiger!

Is . . . no . . . one . . . else at . . . home? Teeth chattering, he manages to utter.

Still trying to growl.

Look, I can't lie to you, I felt like humming a little tune then, only it would have seemed so awful—he was so bloody weak. Shivering, eyelids drooping, lips dry and white.

Lie down, I help him settle into the bed. A clay doll. I wrap him in the blanket. As I cover him my hands brush his limbs, to make him feel my touch. I can count his bones, that's how skeletal he has become.

He's utterly miserable, he wants me to leave. But he doesn't want to be alone either.

Ooh, his helplessness.

I pull up a chair and sit down near him.

The pill will start to act, sleep will come to him, and without the help of a woman's body!

I could see him sinking helplessly as if the pill was a bulldozer and sleep a deep pit.

Shall I say, I wondered, *go to sleep, relax, I'm leaving now, you can keep your arrogance intact, but don't worry, I'll keep checking that all is well.*

He had fallen asleep. No longer aware of my presence or absence. Useless, ill-tempered, ill, proud, cantankerous, devastated.

I could leave.

Or I could keep sitting there.

Suddenly it's rising again, like a silent tornado in me, all the misery of my life, knotting itself into a tight ball. Tighter and tighter it knotted itself.

Confront me who dares, someone, anyone, dare to face me! I'd throw myself at you and grab you tight, break, tear, but not fully demolish, just enough to feel my own power, just enough that your eyes should plead with me in terror and pain, tear you to pieces, claw at the pieces, hear you sob, see you in agony . . .

And then. Indifferently shake you off. Shoo.

54

If you let yourself feel fear even once, it becomes a habit. Just once let go of fear, and then that becomes the habit!

How the days turned around!

That I could scold him like that: 'Go inside!' How you glare at me!

You too want to blame me.

You think he didn't want me to yell at him? You think it wasn't deliberate, his creeping up to the door? Abandoned in his bed, not a soul to ask after him, in all that desolation only me to rush up at his slightest sound, and tick him off. It brought back a spark into that lifeless house.

And his overriding purpose, to deride my audacity in claiming equality with his son. There I am, arguing with Ma: *I have the same desires, the same questions, Ma, that's where I want to go too.* His rising from his bed and lurking by the wall, is his way of saying now stop your devious arguments!

Ma was done with crying. The box had reached its proper place. Now when she was worried, she expressed her anxiety in restrained words, with a new control over her expressions.

'Why *there*? Why this same obstinate insistence?' Yes I was worrying her, but . . .!

How can I explain the sweet sweet taste of worrying her? To have her scold me, thinking of him separately, me separately, thinking of us as separate beings, but joining us in a common complaint. Never before—oh in this long life of mine this was the first time—had it happened thus!

Oh, how my tongue was nimble! 'Don't link everything up to him.'

I knew Father's ears were perking up.

'You know . . .' Ma about to present an argument.

'I know. What happened. The times were different, he was different.'

Me mature, me compassionate, me the hero!

'What did he do wrong? What was his mistake?' Ma remained calm.

Father is bubbling with rage. How dare he, that's me, talk about his son? His intentions so noble, and he, that's me, about to pollute them. Tottering, he stood at the door, about to fall, his stance saying *stop that, look this way, come and attend to me.*

'Isn't it enough that I don't want you to go? I will not let you go.' Ma's voice is firm. She gave me a little slap, soft as love.

Initially I started stammering. Then I just kind of collapsed. Just melted. All tearful.

'Why can't I go there really why, is it only your son who has roots there, maybe I'll learn something too . . .?'

'Learn what?' Ma's eyes are panicky.

I place my hand on her knee. Maybe there was a curiosity somewhere, hidden under the surface, that made my heart restless? And once the thought slipped in, the restlessness began to grow.

The study door made low agitated sounds. *Where do these desires come from*, I wondered, turning to Father. Father thinks only his son has the right to ask questions. But perhaps someone else had indeed asked those questions and I was merely seduced by the sound of those words? A conspiracy!

I must go there, come what may, I resolved, walking towards

Father. After all that's where I was found. Is this plant native to those jungles? Or was it brought from somewhere far away, and replanted there? No, not planted, just flung there.

I'll definitely go, my mind decides and holding Father strongly by his shoulders I march him to bed, letting the thread in my heart loop on and on, stringing on it questions from the past and fears of the present, the sorrow, the frustration, the bitterness of those facing me, winding it round and round into a ball in my chest, tighter and tighter, to sit heavily in my chest, as hard as the primordial stone, waiting to rub against something and burst into flame.

'Do you want to catch pneumonia?' I scold him, but gently.

55

Don't look at me like that please—accusations crowding your eyes! Listen to what I have to say. My life is short, but really long too and maybe I'm not successful, but I've not been unsuccessful either.

Listen to what I'm going to say, hatred is powerful. It can raze mountains, burn trees, lock all the oxygen into Europe and America and create worm-filled gutters elsewhere! And it is hatred that can produce a Hitler, not out of uncivilized, primitive races, nor in times backward and regressive, but in modern prosperous countries at the forefront of the world. Out he went to conquer the universe and crushed all he chanced upon under his boots, and when the foolish world arrived to block his progress, hatred alone gave him the guts to whip out a pistol and shoot himself, and with him Eva Braun! Hatred is proud—its head may be bloody but it's unbowed.

And love? Listen to what I have to say about it. I'll tell you looking deep into your eyes, don't misunderstand! Love is like a tiny little bird, love makes you tiny, insignificant. Breaks your ego, brings you to your knees. You are wounded, your body tormented. Your skin becomes porous like a sieve, and through every pore seep in kindness and sympathy, opening up torrents of blood, of tears, and you start flagellating yourself with all of the hatred you had for the world.

You will say I fell asleep in order to give him pneumonia. Off I nodded, on it came.

But listen. Or don't, but I'm looking straight into your eyes, lovingly, and I'm telling you everything. It's true that I had begun to enjoy wiping his helpless body with a wet towel, and also true that immediately afterwards I carelessly dozed off. But you can't say that's what brought the pneumonia barging in. Like, *here's this wet body, where can it escape, pounce on it.*

The problem, my love—don't mind my using that expression, it just happened in the flow of speaking, like anybody might say to anyone at all, sweetie, darling, honey, love, sugar—the problem is love.

The world is in transition. It hasn't yet turned fully around. So there are forests and gardens made of plastic and rexine in backward countries, all ready for the future—*so what did trees look like, this is what trees looked like*—but real trees survive too, still; trees with real leaves and flowers which grow, which rot.

And still to be found is love, roaming around entranced amidst the villainies of hatred. Wondering where to go.

Love that fills him up so, where is he to spill it, this is what makes Father ill. His son is no more, I am not worthy, Ma rejects it, other women are in pieces, but love bursting out of his heart! He wants to tear to shreds the world that tore his son to shreds. The ball of hatred that blasted his son, he wants to blast the world with it. Revenge! Blood for blood! Destruction for destruction!

But you know, when this man looks at the world with hatred, it's love that oozes out. Bitter and resentful he turns away, frets at his sentimentality.

Now, listen to me, you know what happens then? This longing to hate coils back on him and he begins to hate himself! *What a filthy worm I am, creeping, crawling, loathsome, I can neither kill nor be killed, food comes my way and I begin to eat, my mouth even enjoys soothes me to sleep.*

His, meaning mine. His hand, meaning my hand!

I too began to feel drowsy and dropped off. Father lumbered up from under his blanket, opened the door, went out where it was bitterly cold, sat on the chilly stone, without any cover, in a flimsy vest that welcomed the cold: *come claw me.*

56

No, you have not made your entry yet and my senses are afloat because my eyes have barely opened and how do I know that a cold wave is approaching to engulf Father, that he is sitting out in the open intending to strike up a bond of hate with anything at all, even with himself, a creature so disgusting that anybody would be repelled.

It's not as if he thought this through with a clear mind. But minds are of three kinds: one is a bore, one insane, and one smart, like the milkman who knows the exact proportion of water he can add to the milk! When the bore thinks, his thoughts are unremarkably familiar, the milkman does not think, just sells as quick as he can, and as for the insane mind, whatever thoughts enter it play hide and seek with the one whose mind it is. So it's quite likely that father did not know what he was doing.

And I don't know where Father is. I had packed off Ma to bed, who had been applying cold compresses to his burning forehead, and then dropped off myself while sitting on guard, and now his bed is empty!

I mean, really, does it run in the genes of this family to be present one moment and gone the next?

I opened my eyes and shut them, opened and shut them, jumped clumsily up from the chair, switched on the light, peeped into the bathroom, looked below the bed in case he had rolled off, felt the blanket, is he stuck flat beneath it and then *Ma, Ma*—whirling like a cyclone.

Everywhere. Ma and I. Under every leaf, behind every stone.

It did not occur to me then to wonder if a bomb had been invented with a silencer on it? Nor did it strike me to go outside and check.

A fine specimen of shivering feverish humanity had vanished!

That night was one of bafflement.

The world still slept and we turned the house upside down. What next?

Ma sat down.

I thought she must be thinking that she wouldn't survive if anything happened to him. Must be thinking why did she go to snatch some sleep? Why did she trust careless me?

Ma, I started explaining, see this was how I placed my chair and this was how I sat. Only for a moment I got up to fetch a glass of water, and then I checked the time. I couldn't have dropped off for more than twenty minutes. And he was lying there, honestly, I saw him. And I was thinking I'd go tomorrow to get the racket repaired, the gut strings are all loose . . .

Nonsensical babbling.

'He must be near here, it's unlikely he would have gone very far.' Ma consoling me!

'He doesn't even go jogging.' I'm out of my mind!

But at the mention of jogging, we both have the same thought. Like arrows we shoot out to the front door.

Why is it that when you lose something, it always turns up in the last place you check? Father sat just outside the door, biting the cold and bitten by it.

Ma stood watching patiently. I lifted him in my arms and brought him inside. Now nothing jerks Ma out of her equanimity.

She dusted out the bed sheets and the blanket, and I, Father's clothes. No bomb, not death, but pneumonia. Like a broken branch he swooned on me.

I laid him down.

Low breathing, high fever. We did all we could. It was nearly morning, the doctor was about to come, Ma knew first aid and I knew how to help her.

For a split second Father opened his eyes and gurgled thickly though the spittle collected in his mouth: 'How long will you carry on living, shameless one?'

To me?

But just then he added: '*This* shameless one,' hitting his forehead hopelessly.

57

It lay still in the future, the day of your coming, but our longing for that day had begun to grow.

That morning Ma said, 'Go for your run, there is still time for him to wake and I will look after him till the doctor arrives.'

'Don't let him get up,' I warned, at which she smiled. 'If you leave the room, bolt his door from outside.'

I was not joking. If anything I was extra serious that day. In that mood I could not bring myself to jog so I started on a normal morning walk.

The morning air's not bad and the clouds trapped between buildings give the impression of hills. When the breeze flows, it sings.

This was nothing else but your impending arrival singing in my insane heart, but I did not know. So I walked on, serious, a little tired and sleepy too.

I stop under the tree. I'm not panting today, so it could not have been to catch my breath. But when was it ever to catch my breath? All of it was the preparation. This is where our first meeting is destined to be. In a morning yet to dawn,

I will stand here and catch my breath and you will ask me the way to my own house! My breaths will jerk out in a sweet sinful stutter and my foolish mind will think it's because I've been running. I will not say, great, you want my own address, from me? No, I'll say, go over that nala and when you come to a crossing, turn there, the number you're looking for is in the fourth building.

But not yet. The day. When you would appear under this tree. This moment is meant only to make desire grow towards that day. Preparing for it.

Let the preparing carry on, and if you still don't appear we will conjure you up. From earth fragrant with rain just fallen, in which our desires stir, you, beautiful woman, will emerge.

But not just yet. Not now at all. Right now, you sleep inside us. Let all those essences gradually merge, combining to produce that mist that will part to reveal you.

Let Father's illness grow so that he yearns for my hatred instead of my care, or for you. Let Ma see my examination result, not bad at all, so that she can say, and keep repeating, I *knew* some day . . . but look, there's no question of going there, forget it. Let me say to her, why should I forget it, and have I ever asked you for anything before?

Very soon all this is to happen and everyone's desire to die or to live will converge in an attempt to create you as they please. Come, please come, all unknowing we will beseech you with our yearning hearts.

You're silent. We have not yet seen you. You have seen us from afar, from the guest house of the educational institution, watched us crossing the maidan towards the memorial. You may not have managed a close look at our faces but recognize well the flickering of Ma's shawl.

About me, you know nothing! That there has arrived inside my chest something tense, coiled up and round, which is alive, waiting, to spring on someone like a sweet little child, or a wild beast, or a cloud or lightning, I don't know which, nor does it, nor do you!

And so the preparing carries on, and things advance in such a way that wherever you are, you can no longer stay there, and we drag your feet to the shade of that tree and you will ask a panting eighteen-year-old youth for an address and he does not know that he will speak now as he never has before and that will be the dawning of the day.

58

The doctor examines him thoroughly and goes away. On his prescription writes pneumonia, antibiotics, paracetamol. We are told to look after ourselves and murmuring *yes yes*, into his mobile, *I'll be there in fifteen minutes*, he leaves for the hospital.

Leaving behind Father with chattering teeth, who when he was not racked by coughing, seemed half-dead. When the cough did come upon him, it was never-ending, with smelly greenish phlegm that sprayed on me as well.

'Go,' Father would say, and start to cough again.

'Go,' when he tried to shout, it came out like an out-of-tune note from a broken-stringed instrument. And he vomits.

A stink in the room and the lips of the patient blue and his face looks like shit.

That's pneumonia! Cough, vomit, pain, fever. Can't eat, constipated. Maddened by helplessness, but can't even complain.

The germs roaming free in the air had first settled in his throat. Waiting for a flu to make him weak, so they could begin to gnaw away at his lungs, and then—fever, cough, vomiting.

But these times belong not to the gods but to humans. God may have made the germs and the disease, but humans pick them up with tongs and fling them off. Nothing will happen to Father, he'll be fine in a few weeks.

This is only a germ made by God, not a bomb made by men!

Father feels cold. He can't eat anything.

Ma changes the wet compresses on his forehead. Covers up his chest and neck again and again.

I rub his soles to warm them. He opens his eyes, closes them. Drifts in and out of sleep.

'Who is it who comes here so early in the morning?' He mutters irritatedly to Ma.

Ma feels bad for me. *What do you mean who? Your son.* Drifts off again, neither conscious, nor unconscious.

I support his frame with my arm to make him sit up and take his medicine. Ma gives him water.

Swallow, I say.

He looks rebellious and flops back.

Fathers are not scared of mothers, fathers are scared of sons, fathers are scared of sons who remind them of their son!

His eyes are shut and he's grumbling, *God knows who he thinks he is, landing up to force medicine down my throat.*

His lips and nails had turned blue with the shortage of oxygen. His lungs are in the control of the disease.

I clean up the puke and phlegm.

In revulsion and anger Father says, 'Get out.' Tells Ma, get rid of him.

Where is my son, he asks the ceiling. In his sleep he says, my son is dead.

For about a week we nursed him night and day. Finally he started recovering. His delirium receded.

'I'm fine now. Stop the medicine,' he said to Ma, though it was I giving him his medicine.

'You have to complete the course. Another two weeks.' I pushed his head back.

He said nothing to me. Hid the pills in his mouth. Ma found them on the floor later.

'You'd better swallow or I'll really have to force you, next time I won't let go of your head till . . .' I held on tightly.

'Show me, open your mouth.'

Aaa, he opened his mouth. The pill was gone. But under his tongue this time!

'I see,' I said coldly. Made him swallow it.

Next time. I was making the bed and found it under the pillow.

We confronted each other every time. *If I need to, I'll tie up your hands, I will pour buckets of water down your throat to make you swallow, don't be under any illusion.*

He began to cough. I rubbed his chest hard. *But look, the moment a drop of sweat appears, you throw off the covers. How will you ever get well?*

I grumble angrily when we are alone together, 'You know I have other things to do, I have to prepare for my move to another town, to study at that university and here I am on duty twenty-four hours of the day!'

'Finish me off,' he mutters. To whom, I wonder.

Yes, Father wants to die. He wants to make himself repellent with stench and filth. He wants to bring the hatred he had failed to bring to his own eyes, into the eyes of the one in front of him. I massage his chest and feet and back, but he doesn't want to feel better, doesn't want my hands to bring him relief, doesn't want to want me to continue.

But I keep on doing it and he begins to sink into his weakness, to grow you in a dream. Come, redeem him, free him from my custody.

59

It really wasn't too bad, I mean, if you look at it as coming from a *non-performer*, it certainly proved all doubts and fears to be baseless; it was an excellent result! So much so that it filled Father with new strength to say to all who would listen that these days there is no relation between how you write the exam and what marks you get; do it well and you might fail, do an indifferent job and you might top, anything can happen, really.

Ma patted me gently. 'I knew that one day you would,' she said.

I was happy. I had never hoped for this. In fact, I had never acquired the habit of hoping for anything at all in the years of my growing up. But when the result turned out to be fine, hopelessness became a thing of the past. That morning I shaved and doused myself in aftershave lotion. Then I gave Ma a hug.

Hope is a cunning thing, though. For long she had been building up resentment at my indifference. Look at this fellow, untouched by me, unperturbed, contentment on his face like a sage in the forest! Like it's all the same to him if he lives or dies. Passes or fails. Natha Singh or Prem Singh, one and the same thing! Okay, here's how to get him. Shine up his result a little. Goddess of fortune, listen to me. Shine up his result and then watch how I'll set up somersaults inside of him. He'll wander around as if in a dream, his breathing uneven.

Well, that's exactly what happened!

His friends would come to look up Father and I would excitedly tell them that I had sent off for the admission form. I felt like saying to them that their friend was my role model.

'Surely you can understand,' I said to them. 'This is what your friend wanted, too.'

We'd get to debating his wishes heatedly. Father listening from his room, Ma sitting among us, turning from one face to the other and us young folk excitedly discussing his hopes, his questionings.

That's where I have to go. To see for myself what's going on. Shooting the unarmed, imagine!

His reflections once. Now mine.

Newspapers are filled with reports of that time. And things are no different now.

I had underlined an eye-witness account, read it out to them, see: *Why did they shoot at me, I was doing nothing, I had no weapon, and the whole army and the government chasing after one innocent person! See, here's where one bullet hit me, and here another. Why?*

Really, why? I must go there, I must figure this out.

He used to say this too. It's our world, we should figure out the logic of this stuff.

If you talk so much about one who has gone, his spirit enters the very air, and his form starts to get filled in by us, like a fictional character.

I say 'fiction' but I don't mean a lie—fiction in the sense that there are no demands for proof, no obstacle to the narrative, no limits set by science or history. He himself starts to speak, slipping out of our grasp and recreating himself as he pleases. What floated abstractly in the mind becomes concrete—from his mind to mine, from mine to his and all these questions are mine too, going off like bombs, so innocently, inside me.

Father walks in. Ma knows his expression. He's about to lose his temper, I know this. Ma wants me to stop before it gets awkward. I felt like I was there again, where the bomb had wreaked its destruction but this time not I, but he—he, not I—was lying in that empty space, lying forgotten, nobody thinks of him, it's me they all want to touch, to hold, to interrupt, to stop, to sidetrack!

The longing deepens.

In their longing, my longings too had grown. Like when you water spinach, the *bathua* sprouting between the furrows gets water too!

Oh the longing.

You. Where are you?

60

We were all beginning to miss you!

You think I'm joking. The meeting hasn't happened, but the missing has begun!

But that's it exactly. It's a disease, this habit of those who build chronologies, to fix everything, stabilize everything, in one straight sequence. This is how things are, this is how things happen. A beginning, a middle, an end. First strangers, then acquaintances, then the missing . . .! Topsy, then turvy.

Why not 'that' first, then 'this'? Death first, life afterwards. Result first, admission later. The practice, then the theory, the game then the rules, and the elephant then Ganesh!

Because this is how it is, there is no sequence and what there is, is something else quite extraordinary. Like your eyebrows and the head of Ganesh.

Okay, tell me, did Ganesh perform austerities pleading for an elephant head as a boon? But who would have worshipped him if he didn't have an elephant head? Is Kartikeya worshipped? Not in a big way, *na*? So damn logic and order, and figuring out who came first, the elephant or Ganesh, just take it as gospel truth that had Ganesh been left with his own head, he too would have joined the ranks of *non-performers* and you'd better believe this too, that devotees, desperate to love him, would have found something else to adorn him with, had there been no elephant, like maybe elongated, bow-shaped eyebrows, joined in the middle! Like yours!

So add to the list of gospel truths that had you left these maddening eyebrows at home, we would have found some other amazing feature to stamp you with! Blinded you in one eye, or painted one half of your body. To make you a deity worth worshipping!

And so we summoned you there, under that tree and you came along with the bow arched above your eyes, and shot your arrow into our three hearts. Adorable girl, made from our longings, who came from the very place to which I proposed to go, and your sweet words will gradually dilute the poison of the place for Father, and Ma could say *you know every corner of that place and the killings and violence, you can stop him, forbid him.* She doesn't add, *because he's just mesmerized by you, follows you like a devoted puppy, happy with the smallest morsel or pat from you, following you around, love me, shoo me, tickle me, my lovely girl!*

Lovely girl! Of course.

Whether you are present or not, it's you to whom I speak, to whom I'll keep speaking.

Like Ma and Father do, too.

It does happen sometimes that someone comes along, to become so truly one's own.

This is how I shall be forever now, addressing you in all I say, whether you're here or not. My speaking cannot end now, even if you do!

I have said it before, and shall say it again, that there are people who need a listener in order to speak and a reader in order to write and a bracelet maker for their wrists to tinkle. But I don't, trust me.

With me, it's the opposite. I'll fall silent—or feel like it—if a face appears before me, listening, head tilted to one side, eyes piercing, judging me. My tongue will stutter and my fingers will drum nervously and I'll hurry to complete my thoughts, *am I managing to say what I wanted to say, am I making a fool of myself?* My ears like a tuner, a synthesizer, catching every false note, every discordant tone, trying desperately to save the situation, and to render it all tuneful.

Nahin, no, without a doubt, I am far happier when there is no one before me to listen and to tell me that I've lost it, that I'm wayward.

Life is like that. It makes us wayward.

Does having a face in front of you mean an audience? I have my doubts. Suppose I was speaking in a jam-packed hall. What I'd do is, turn them all off and switch on only you, somewhere in all that crowd. You can imagine what I'd do after that. It could be the world's most serious topic I'd be pontificating on—Naxalites, racists, colour, gender, murders, lootings, whatever—even at that gravest of grave moments, I'll do what I have to. Once I see you in the crowd, away I'll go, swinging along my own voice flung across like a rope, sliding down it like an acrobat to where you are. And gathering you in my arms I shall place my lips on yours and dart my tongue into your left cheek, then your right, like lightning. Then go sliding down your body to do the same—left cheek then right—storming you with my tongue.

Leaving behind the clash of civilizations!

No, audience, readers, viewers, will solve nothing. Certainly won't solve waywardness.

No, certainly not waywardness, which comes from never being in one place and from a place never remaining the same.

This was my attempt. This was what I tried with you. To fill you with everything that was mine. Everything that was scattered around so far, all the pieces, gather them in you. Become one. In one place.

But instead what happened was that when I loaded you with my pieces, you fell to pieces. The scattered shards tore into you.

Nothing joined up. No. Not yours, not mine. Only wind and rain and sticks and glass and waywardness.

All of it in turmoil inside this body, which looks deceptively poised, balanced, coordinated.

61

The heart is growing impatient, it longs to soar over the intervening space and land its aircraft in that morning. *Voh subah kabhi toh aayegi.* For that dawn must break sometime. Why not today?

It came.

It was a beautiful morning.

For the last time I locked Father in before leaving so that Ma could let him out, otherwise just to bug me he was quite capable of wandering outside in his netted vest, coughing away, inviting his pneumonia back, *aa laut ke aa ja,* oh return, beloved pneumonia, my self-loathing calls you back!

In that beautiful morning, eddies of fog were billowing.

You won't believe me. You'll say I'm on a romantic trip and adding my own colour to bleak reality. But I will still hold that there was fog, it was beautiful, and if it hadn't been there, it should have been, and so there was!

I kept running on my usual route, and the wind ran with me. Now look, of this there is proof. Of the sort you people accept. The papers reported that a cyclone hit the city and roofs were lifted off.

Of course, I didn't know this. Ours was not the kind of roof that would fly off in storms and as for me, I was in such a state those days that I wouldn't notice even if it had. If one is in flight oneself, one doesn't notice what else is in the air. Or you might think it's your own eyes making everything seem to be afloat!

The wind was turning wild, this I saw. Buffeting itself restlessly against the earth, I saw. I saw waves begin to leap in the gutter. Never before had I experienced a wind so intense that if you stood before its flow, it would carry you along with it, helplessly jogging at full speed! Along the gutter, it was so powerful it could lift you up, fill your clothes out and for a few moments suspend you in midair, next to Trishanku, clang you like a bell and then drop you, plop, right into the water.

Headlines would say: he parachuted down into the waters! But I was lost in the melody of my own youth. Why should I let myself be carried along *with* the wind? Why not uproariously *against* it? I flung my arms out as if to stop the wind, to stop you. Road closed! It would retreat, I would advance upon it, slapping it along.

And this is how I reached under our tree where the leafy branches began to tap their tuneful dance upon my head.

It was the wind, you'll say. It was you, I'm telling you!

I notice that someone has flung a fistful of fog into the wind, which has spread over the sky like a djinn. And as the djinn lowers his head in a salute, you emerge down the road.

From afar, a delicate melody. Approaching closer. You went on becoming Ganesh, I went on creating you, you won't believe this.

No elephant head, but eyebrows that meet in the middle, like a long, black bow above the eyes. The image that now rules my mind.

You just refuse to believe it. You say I did not even notice you and was busy waiting for the storm to abate, and was turning away to leave when you called out—a moment please.

How do I convince you? I did see you, and the moment I saw you, something happened. I felt something happening that was inevitable, fated; I was shaken, I looked around in a daze. That's what it was.

Yes. A moment please. On this we are both agreed! Also that I turned and answered your question about where our house is.

You have asked me this, *if you were so struck by meeting me, why didn't you come home with me? Why did you return to your jogging and on getting home, not even recognize me and just go straight up to your room?*

Because, that's how it is. This is that very thing that floats about in the air, shooting out suddenly like a mosquito and alighting on the skin, giving you a little bite that you cannot feel, injecting anaesthesia into you, sitting there sucking your blood, *that's it that's it*, ringing in your blood but you are unconscious of it, you keep jogging, return home, she is there before you, but the anaesthesia is still in your blood, you look around blankly, go upstairs, and then the malaria hits you, but hey, when did the mosquito bite?

When I saw the black curved bow. And then I could never stop seeing it!

62

So which story should be believed, yours or mine? Everyone else agrees with you, you claim. You are the majority, I am the minority.

If the majority is always right, what's happening all around us is right. It's right to desire a fridge and nuclear arms and limitless power. Just a few remain, who are satisfied with forests, with sun and thatch, small desires and little smiles, they must be wrong. Here I am, insisting that one look at you and I was floored, but you insist that I was smug and callow, absorbed in myself over the days and nights.

According to you I seemed utterly self-obsessed at home whenever you saw me, offering you the obligatory greeting, but after that, so very busy busy!

How much can I protest and deny, and to how many? Let's drop this point and move on.

Every day she's started coming home, this new girl. Right? Ma pats her cheek and Father places his hand on her head. Not lecherously, but in blessing. This very girl now gives him his medicines, sometimes pulls him out by his hand and brings him into the front room. The three of them sit and chat.

You never noticed us, so how would you know what we were talking about, you hit out.

But anyone would want to talk to you, the way you listen to everyone, with such love! Why would I be surprised by that?

What you should wonder about is why I didn't mind. The three of you, separate from me. Well, that's because I knew it was only your kindness, your courtesy. After doing your bit for the old ones, you'd come to me, to me alone, to ask me, about myself, to make me tell my story, with such tenderness.

You lie. Even to yourself. You chide me lovingly.

You say it was much later that you started coming up to me. That I have put in the beginning what came afterwards.

Hey, what's all this about beginning and end, in romance there's no such thing.

But you insist I was not interested. That I would never have been interested, if Ma had not fought with me.

Again? You had said entering at that moment. What? I had replied, surprised.

You and Ma are fighting again? How do you know, I asked.

I know Ma's face, you smiled. Purple with rage, I too smiled.

That was the moment we became friends, you say. Well, thank god you accept we became friends!

But that was a special moment for me. Do you know why? Ma said, exhausted, 'Explain to him why it's a bad decision to go there.'

Where? You asked.

You were the first person who knew nothing about me and would be interested in everything about me. You were the first one not to know that I'm the one who's in his place.

The first to look at me, only me, in my own shape, and with my own shadow!

'Oh, that university's in my state!' you said. I learnt that for the first time

Oh, I responded.

That was the first time I noticed you with any interest, you say. Although I say it was then I felt even more certain that this one was made for me, I knew it when I first set eyes on those eyebrows!

'How is it there?' I asked. Desiring it more, now that I knew you belonged there.

'How is it there?' Ma scolded again. 'Tell him please!'

'But why only there?' you asked, innocently.

Knowing nothing of my connection to that place, who I was and who I wasn't. I am, I'm today, not the past, not the ghost of someone else!

I liked that.

63

Don't get all prickly if I call it love. The air is romantic and playful, everything is love, everyone is in love. The house is joyous and inside Ma and Father too, beats the breathless rhythm of anticipation.

But don't even dream of matching the exuberance of eighteen years. When you fall in love at eighteen it's so intense, each memory of even its incomplete moments brings back that season again! The days are languorous, the heart is eighteen, and love snakes inside you like electricity.

Do you understand? No, of course not.

No way you can get it. Because you did not fall in love at eighteen. That's why you don't have those filaments of energy inside you, coiling into a round ball of life, ready to pounce. They stretch and stretch languorously, producing an empty space waiting to be filled; you have no idea what that feels like. No idea of the novel vision of that empty space which says, here is the very beginning, free of all that is old and musty, waiting for everything to start from this point on, fragrant and fresh!

None of you can compete with me. All of you have left eighteen behind. Lost the chance.

This day is mine to live, and to create, which is the same thing.

I jogged, firmed up my biceps and triceps under the tree, and I came back home to you, bringing you pieces of the open sky; today I will be happy.

Breakfast, I shouted. Then I saw you and felt a little sheepish. So early today? Hid my excitement.

You had been somewhere with Ma.

Your office was open this early? I asked Ma casually and went upstairs to spruce up.

You will look at my face, let my face become a means to give you pleasure!

Even Father did not get up to leave at my coming down. Your arrival had changed all that.

Ma content that we all sat together. Even if we didn't speak to each other. What was the need for that anyway? It's you everyone wants to talk to!

A little fruit juice spills out of my glass. I wipe it quickly with a napkin before you notice my clumsiness. I want to look elegant in your eyes.

You said something. To Ma or to Father.

I didn't hear. You keep saying something or the other to them anyway.

But an elastic band has joined me to you and through you to this world. I swoop and arch, now this way, now that. Sometimes we swoop, sometimes the world. The whirling dance of the dervish, the suppleness of this band!

Ma laughed. So did Father. Laughter in these ruins!

I got up with my coffee and went to my room.

No haste in me. Romance is not a thing to hurry up, it must be savoured slowly. You will come. You come each time. To say bye. Or at Ma's bidding, *go get some sense into his foolish brain, there's a university here too*. But don't tell me you didn't have any interest of your own in me?

You enjoy my conversations, don't you? I joke, I take off, giving sage-like sermons. At which you smile. *It's not like that*, you shake your head gently disagreeing. You do that deliberately, don't you? Like heroines through the centuries, to let sweet tendrils of hair caress your cheek?

Then I may make use of one tiny drop of the vast ocean of courage roaring inside me! With the very tip of my finger, brush back that lovely strand and let your cheek rest, *so*, on my finger; if you were to shake it off, you would fall without its support, weightlessly, helplessly.

You turn your head aside.

So many times have you said to me: I ask you so many questions, why don't you ask about me?

Yaaron mujhe maaf karo, mein nashe mein hun! Intoxication has me in her grip, my friends, I beg forgiveness!

'What do you know about me yet,' I snap. 'Do you even know that I was there where the bomb exploded?'

I see her face lose colour and my heart can win a high jump competition!

64

Like this, I lay down on the floor and showed her. We were alone in my room upstairs.

Just us and between us, my passionate ravings. No one else dare enter. Throw them out, and if they protest, blow them up with a bomb! This is how it is today, have you any idea how many blasts take place year upon year?

I pulled her down on the floor beside me.

This is how I lay there. I remember, I said. Curling up foetally, to make my eighteen evoke three. *Above me fans whirred, all greasy and mucky, ready to fall on me. I felt scared.*

I turned to look at her. She was resting on her elbow looking at me. Listening to me attentively. Looking at me carefully.

Wouldn't you have been scared? I long for her sympathy. Three years old, lying alone and abandoned, staring at the fans? Would anyone ever have been in my plight?

Emerging from such a calamity, I was enjoying showing off my wounds to her. What a story, and what a hero am I! And listening to me, my heroine.

The devastation of bombs and the desperation to charm her.

'The position you're lying in makes all the difference,' my voice has thickened. 'The best position to spy on the world is to be flat on the ground, and not have to worry about getting admission. No anxiety in your mind about exams, just lying there with nothing to do, looking all around, who is coming in, who is going out, someone holding an admission form, someone a bomb.'

'What a lot of nonsense you talk,' she said. A little scared. I liked it.

'He was there,' I said. 'Now you know about him. We were both there.'

She followed my eyes and both of us looked at the photograph. On the bookshelf. At such an angle that though it was we who turned to him, it seemed as if *he* had strained his neck towards the floor!

'He was sitting there,' I wove a story. 'Legs crossed. Gulping down his coffee. Nervous about his exam, shaking one leg insistently. Slip-on shoes. One had fallen, and lay under the table.'

She looked at me in disbelief. Panic on her face. Sympathy in her heart.

'If you're stretched out like this, it's the kind of thing you see. Below the table, shoes, slippers, some on feet, some on the floor. Tremors of the leg revealing the state of the head! Who is restless, who a dandy, who devil-may-care, who with a chip on his shoulders! And listen, shall I continue,' I asked.

She nodded yes, but said nothing.

'The sandals of the waiters flapping. This is it, the time to make a fast buck. Once these youngsters write their entrance exams, they'll be sahibs, out of our orbit.'

She was looking at me numbly. What a way to tell the story! Where bombs explode one does not joke. Most inappropriate to recount it lightly, airily. This discourse on shoes and slippers, what sense does it make?

But I was in my own flow. Started talking about high heels. That the girls wore.

'Girls like you wear high heels. Some, like you, do social work, some just fashionably sit around in cafes drinking coffee.'

Now she looked convinced I was crazy.

'Crazy,' I said.

'You?' She barely whispered.

'The bomb,' I said in a changed voice.

'You saw?' She asked, when I went quiet.

'Did I see? Did I recognize its footwear? Pure export-quality leather? Or cracked cheap plastic slippers from the weekly market? Walking in hatred carrying a sack hiding the bomb! Why does the sack move so? *Bori-wale, ay, teri bori mein kya hai? Bori mein hai taqdeer hamari!* O sack-wala mine, what holds your sack? It holds, what it holds, is our fates!'

'You asked?' how sad she was.

Nobody asked. So many clever guys there, not one asked. Who is this, who dares say he belongs here, and we are aliens? The border, always another border. This is mine, my burrow, my religion, my village, my gutter, my bomb.

'And it exploded?' Tearfully.

I just lay there. Started looking at myself. Embers, dismembered limbs, flying slippers, shoes, sandals, heels, soles, straps, buckles, tongues, leather . . .

I lay there, tearful myself.

65

So the verdict had been pronounced: we are all to love you! After all, there's love inside all of us. It fills us up, and we never find the one upon whom to pour it. The bomb? It did what it had to do, and pushed off. It was Ma and Father who were devastated—their lives had been devoted to him, and now what? They turn to me, and he comes all entangled with me. Life gets all entangled—he is, is not; I am, am not.

You're an angel. So uncomplicated, even Father was smitten, no? Ma's mother-love of course, is unsurpassed.

The fact that you and Ma worked together at her social work organization worked out great for me.

I didn't feel bad about their loving you. To have Ma and Father adore you worked in my favour. For the first time in my life I was turning into a hero, a hero freed by a beautiful woman; freed, elevated, cajoled, charmed. Everything about me enchants you. And that made me alluring to myself.

Now I'm never alone even when alone. At all times your warmth, at every moment the thrill of imagining what you would see if you were looking at me, what my words would sound like to your ears; if you inhaled my soul, what a sigh would arise from it.

From a *non-performer* I had become a *performer*.

I was standing outside in the light of the dawn. Imagining you inside the house. The door is closed, soon you would leave with Ma to her office to carry on with the research that brought you here, but you would wait, you would meet me.

I remembered something about our last meeting and smiled, and imagined that you smiled along with me. Inside, on the other side of the door, in the middle of saying something to Father or Ma. You would have been a little embarrassed, thinking *they'll wonder what I'm smiling at*.

It made me laugh.

Would she know I laughed? In her imagination I must be here, by the side of the nala. The sun, rose-pink, slanted onto the water and on my cheeks. She would see me and say, *putting on airs like a hero*.

I imagined her imagining me walking like this. She says, *why do you look like that, always something going on in your mind?* I'll tell you what's going on in my mind, I'll tell you everything. To you, to whom else?

But now look at me. Coming towards the house. You like my toned body, don't you? Surely she wants to touch me. Surely one day she won't be able to stop herself, falling . . .

Something live lurches in my chest, scurries to another part of my body, mischievously.

I'm embarrassed. She should never know. How my thoughts fly around! I started walking more carefully. I must look serious, nothing else. Standing at the door, she should see me approach. She's recognizing me from my walk. A small piece of gravel in my shoe. With great style I lift a foot, pull off my shoe, shake it out, wear it again. A dancer, an athlete.

There are flowers on the way. I don't yet have the courage to give you some. You tease me in my mind—*coward!* Just you wait, one day I'll get you. Go on, laugh!

I stop by the woman selling earthen pots. Watching myself with your eyes, I pick up a surahi. *Is it for me?*—I hear your teasing voice. I put it back and walk on empty-handed.

The young man stands outside the house. You must be seeing him in your mind. Or out of a window. You're keeping a check on your excitement: *he will come in and I'll look up casually but in my heart I will devour him.*

Imagining all of this my walk has become self-conscious. I enter the house trying to look normal and find there's no one about!

Meaning you hadn't come today.

Meaning wherever you are today you will see me in your mind, whatever I do, I'll see you looking at me, I will look good, I'll be adorable, awkward, I'll look an ass!

But I'll laugh and wait for you to come tomorrow.

66

You'll come. My heart turns cartwheels. Downstairs you'd help out, chat a little. I'll wait. Won't be able to bear the waiting. I'll come to the stairs. You'll say hello. When did you come, I'll say smilingly. Coming downstairs to everybody, but there's only you and me really, I'll revel in us. Then I'll go up again so that Ma would send you after me: *go, he talks to you, listens to you, such an introvert, he used to stay shut up in his room up till now*. You would come to my room, as if only at her bidding! As if it is nothing to you. My stories, I. Which you persuasively make me tell—do you remember, the cafe, the bomb, what did you see, who did you see, what did you feel?

I am Ali Baba with another name! The magic words are not *khul ja simsim* or Open Sesame, Close Sesame, but Open Love, Close Death.

Wrong! In the pages of love, death is present too, swinging on that same elastic band!

I have taken over his desire to go there to the same university, and renewed the same anxiety in everyone. I'm enjoying it.

Ma has put you on the job too—*tell him what you know, talk some sense into him. You know the area, tell him.*

'Are you Ma's bomb, her secret weapon to explode some sense into me?' I tease you. Uncaring about the smile that escapes my lips—the words no longer carry the old hurt. Under your spell everything has become innocent. Joined together.

Ma began her railing at me—*why would she say what I want her to say? Doesn't she have a brain of her own, my girl?*

'No, no, it's me who's brainless. When he said the same thing, he was brainy. Who the hell am I, right?'

'Did he decide so impulsively?' You ask. 'He must have talked about it, asked people for their opinions.'

'Nonsense,' I said. 'You people wouldn't have agreed to discuss it with him either. You'd have done the same.'

Look at me, look how cool I am. My mind a merry-go-round. All my organs wheeling around in joy. My tongue, my hands, my feet too. Spin spinning.

Scold him, Ma says.

I am not scolding you, you say softly.

But you are, I say, not minding, really. Become an announcer I say. You have a great voice. And when scolding it sounds great!

I am *not* scolding you. You scold.

I'm a merry-go-round. I spin merrily. What could I do? I love your voice. But I like your voice. I said it.

What could I do? I liked everything about her. Shall I say it, I like you?

Not yet. It's just the beginning.

Not then. It was the beginning. In the beginning one doesn't say I like you. One says oh, it's raining again.

Meaning I like you. One says, Ma don't keep cleaning my cupboard. Meaning I like you. One says I need to get some eggs. Meaning I like you. Nudge Ma to show her that father was standing about without a sweater and she goes to give him one. But this exchange too, is really about you and me, meaning the same—I like you.

'Are you sure?' I asked. Meaning the same thing!

Ma's cigarette was lit. Father coming this way with his post-pneumonia lungs. I yanked out Ma's cigarette from her mouth and stubbed it out in the ashtray. Smoke curled out. Its wisps say the same thing. I like you.

My tongue spins around some more: Do we think before lifting the right foot and then the left? When we trip and fall do we think, put this hand down first and then that? How much did you think before getting into social work? Did you think or it just came to you? Do we choose what we do or does it choose us? Every year do I think, should I age another year? Is there any alternative? At a crossing it will be either left or right, is there another alternative?

In the exam it will either be pass or fail, is there any other alternative?

I like you I like you uncontrollably spinning.

Ma looking affectionate at my badinage. But thoughtful too.

'Ma, what could he have thought? Can we ever know?'

Unintended words spill out in the whirl of the merry-go-round.

I turned to you. He would have turned eighteen. Would have woken up in the morning. The earth would have been fragrant with moisture. He would have wanted to be an ant and burrow in it. He would have wanted to make friends with the whole world. He would have wanted to bow to all the mothers. To forgive every father. Would have wanted to caress the cheek of every girl. To hum, even tunelessly. To swing on every branch and every leaf. His head would have floated like a cloud and his eyes would have raced in the air to decide where to stay and shower his rain. All around him would have been the vast skies, empty, empty, such space, more space, what a longing must have risen in his soul, let anything, everything . . .

Not that I said all of this! Just fell silent. All serious. All I said was he must have seen the nala in our neighbourhood and must have thought he must dive in, no matter if he drowned.

She looked perturbed. Ma kept quiet.

One drowned, one will dive. I did not say that.

I turned sharply to Ma, 'Don't question me so much that I get confused about whether this is what I want, myself. Or is it someone else's desire? Is it he who wants me to go there? Perhaps. Or is it that *you* want what he wants? Are you sending me on a pilgrimage?'

Ma's silence suddenly grew louder.

That's it, that's it, that's it, goes round and round in my head. Ma and pilgrimage.

67

The air was suddenly very still and Father's coming over to us echoed loudly.

He sat, his back towards me, and started turning over some files.

I shrugged questioningly at Ma, she looked at you and you asked Father what are you looking for?

I'll show you, he said.

His back towards me. Talking to you. Saying, whatever you do, do it with dedication, not all *phoos-phaas phoos-phaas.*

This is for my ears.

The papers in the file rose and fell. How would I have known what they were?

Read. Father says with force. And suddenly without warning, an about-turn towards me! Giving me the papers. Holding the file towards me.

If someone always sits like a wall before you and suddenly a window opens in it, wouldn't you lose your balance a bit?

I was filled with stammering. To suppress it I said with excessive calm—what's this, I'll read it.

When someone who never speaks to you suddenly speaks, and says, jump off a cliff, wouldn't you, in astonishment, just do it?

I opened my mouth to read. Excessively calm. Some pages fell to the ground. I just started to read an open page, whether it was one I picked up or one he handed to me, I can't be certain. It was in English.

> *But that was nothing to what things came out . . . What were they? Mermaids? Dragons? Ghosts? Nothing at all of any things like that*
> *What were they then?*
> *All sorts of queer things*

I read on, mechanically, beginning to recognize the poem by Robert Frost from one of his books.

At some point in my head the message began to tap out—this was his handwriting I was reading.

I read on.

> *Things never seen or heard or written about*
> *Very strange . . . Utterly peculiar*
> *Things. Oh, solid enough they seemed to touch, Had anyone dared it. Marvellous creation,*
> *All various shapes and sizes, and no sizes, All new, each perfectly unlike his neighbour, Though all came moving slowly out together.*

The file is in my hands. Papers, notes that had fallen out, someone had picked them up, given them to me, but I continued to read, blankly, without understanding, with the tap-tap of the message ringing in my ears. I am reading, without understanding.

Describe just one of them
I am unable
What were their colours?
Mostly nameless colours . . .

I'm thinking, tap tap tap how must he feel, this stuff he wrote for himself being touched like this, read like this . . .? Father . . . I . . .

Some had no colour.
Tell me, had they legs?

The pages pour scorn on me. They say *keep quiet.*

. . . They came out on the sand,
Not keeping time to the band, moving seaward
Silently at a snail's pace. But at last
The most odd, indescribable thing of all
Which hardly one man there could see for wonder
Did something recognizably a something. Well, what?
It made a noise.

My voice echoing traitorously in my ears. How must these words he loved sound in my voice?

A frightening noise ?

No, no

Father must be laughing?

A musical noise? A noise of scuffling? No, but a very loud . . .

These people in front of me, are they listening to him or to me? . . . *respectable noise . . .*

I could no longer hear my voice.

68

Whose voice was that? His? Mine? The voice of a small boy.

Tell me, where does the voice of a small boy go?

A small boy gets lost in the desert. Where can his voice go? Does it hover in the air, directionless, purposeless, then return to him?

Tell me, it's you I ask, where do the feelings in the heart of a small boy go? Wander forlornly here and there, and then get trapped in a barren branch. That's all . . .

69

The general mood sort of changed with nothing specific marking it. Just the gleam of victory in Father's eye, seeing me crumble. Making me read his handwriting, kicking me in the butt.

My heart started to mutter *don't get too agitated, what if you can't stand it?*

I had rushed out of the room, you see. Stopped at the stairs. Started climbing slowly. Held back my tears, eyes tightly shut. After a long time I was back to the old rhythm—one, two, three . . . the plant . . . turn here . . . six seven eight . . . room. The old familiar ways are safe, reassuring; new desires terrify.

I went in and lay down quietly on the bed. On his bed.

I could not have imagined it, Father meant to humiliate me. For sure. Because these days I had begun to monopolize the gatherings. I was the topic of discussion. And what's more, it was all in wishes and arguments and expressions 'stolen' from him! No echo of my own. *Will go there, will only go there!* Who the hell do you think you are?

Who knows, I only know that I'm from there too. *I'll go there for sure*, my heart insisted. Maybe something will draw me to that earth. I need to go there at least once. I might find a connection?

Well, one connection has already emerged. You. You live in that area, Ma felt comforted by that. You'd keep an eye on me.

Do watch over me, my heart whispered, in its loneliness. What must you have thought of me rushing out like that? Did you see my tears?

I slept. That tired sleep. I was tired.

If it's not a deep sleep, you dream. The dreams of light sleep. Dreams can be fun. Stories form, break. Dreams don't try to tune the narratives. They enjoy incoherence.

When I woke up it was dusk. My head, my body, felt heavy. If you sleep at the wrong time, you attract ghosts. This was the time for ghosts.

Ma always says, as soon as it's dark turn on the lights. The ghosts will run away.

I lay there, still drowsy. In the dark.

Slowly I began to realize there was someone in the room. Apart from me.

A familiar feeling, I began to remember. My eyes tried to cut through the dark and see the photograph.

Certainly there's someone.

I moved and so did it. At the window, a shadowy body.

This had happened before. I'd thought it was Father. But it was him. He had touched the walls of the house and said goodbye, smelt the flower to lose desire, sipped the water of forgetting. I, the eye witness. I had followed him, seen it all myself.

You could say I dreamt it. I don't really know, was it real or a dream?

I don't know if this is real or a dream? Had I woken up in my dream or woken from sleep in my room?

Who? I made a kind of sound.

The shadow at the window moved. Ma.

Ma? I would have said, but last time I thought it was Father and it turned out to be him. What was truth and what fantasy?

She turned. Those enormous eyes. Even in the dark the curved bow was visible. She opened her arms.

I went into them.

70

Shh, shh, she said. Though we were standing quietly. She knew what Father had done with me. Taken revenge. The shame of my tears was washed away.

Just washed away. We said nothing, we did nothing, we just stood there quietly.

That creature inside me also quiet. No commotion in my chest. Nor anywhere else.

She knew three and eighteen had got entangled and knotted me up.

She had always come up to me after spending a while downstairs, and she did the same today. I was asleep. She waited. It became dark. I woke up. Her arms, soft and caressing, her breath, sweet and soothing.

She knew Ma and Father had entangled three and eighteen in me.

There was no impatience in us, no hurry, a quiet, peaceful embrace.

She did not tangle me up.

I hadn't ever tasted this flavour. To hold so, to be held so.

'I like you,' I said.

She switched on the lights. My eyes blinked at the sudden brightness. I looked at her. She was sad. Like me.

We sat down.

Her mobile phone was peeping out of her bag. I took it out.

Looked at the time. Ma would have gone to feed the dogs. Father would not pick up the phone if I was in the house. I dialled the landline and handed the phone back to her, 'Want to hear his voice?'

She looked scared. Snatched the phone and turned it off. 'I have heard it,' she said, in panic.

'*My going there is also his*,' I said sadly. She was sad too. She said nothing.

Ma really wants me to go there. She tells you to dissuade me only to hide her own desire.

She didn't say anything.

I will go. You'll be there. I won't be scared. You want it, too. This story appeals to you, I know it. It's fast becoming your story. You want to see for yourself what happened where.

As always she let me ramble on.

I tell you everything. I will show you everything. I vowed eternal love.

71

I had finally got something concrete to hold forever against Father, never to forgive him. And that resolved all indecision. My mind was now made up.

It isn't such an unusual way for decisions to crystallize. Big ideas, the curiosity of eighteen, some anxiety, some nonchalance, and suddenly everyone else gives up.

Your visits did not stop but finally the curtain came down on the theatre of cajoling me and dissuading me. Every objection of yours had given me a new argument and on top of it all, there were your eyebrows. Actually we can even pretend that you, Father, Ma, had all been playing at stopping me, while actually laying my doubts to rest!

Those days only one fear remained: what if she didn't come upstairs to meet me? I knew she would but still, would she come or not!

That year, why not say it, was the most important year of my life. How many evenings of that year did I spend in fear—will she come, or not, and when?

Today she has come with Ma, today she's with Father at the topiwala gathering, today she is downstairs, I can hear her chatting. Soon she will make her way up.

I sit with an open book, read a little, stop reading. Let me read a little more, another paragraph, and in the meanwhile, the hands of the clock might move a little.

Her voice trailed up. What do you keep talking about with them, I shall ask again, but don't have patience for the answer. I have so much to say to you, myself. Actually, it is me she is connected to, she connects me to myself, I forget my unhappiness and become a hero.

She liked all my innocent ways and so I did, too. Oh, I never liked myself so much before!

She'll be here any moment. I stop reading and strike poses in the mirror—how do I look when I speak, shall I listen with my fist resting reflectively against my brow, smile rakishly? Intelligent in this pose, so-o-o sexy in this, cute in this one! Do my teeth show, is there spit at the corner of my mouth, dandruff in my hair?

She did not embrace me again after that evening. But there's no hurry. I'm in no hurry. That day will come. The right day, beautiful, opening out, spreading itself, like clouds, lightning and rain. For now, let there be other things, let her come upstairs.

Come *na*, I sulk. I try to read some more but imagine her head bent over the book, reading the same page as me. My attention is less on the page, more on her head.

I draw in a deep breath. *Washed your hair?* I'll ask.

But when will you come? You don't come, and you don't leave me alone, always so deep inside me that I do nothing by myself.

Still chatting with them!

I feel like shouting—hey the ocean of talk will dry up, are you going to come to me with the sand? Shall I say mock-stylishly, ma'am leave us some ocean too!

My heart felt so turbulent that year. There was so much I had to say to her. All that had already been said. All that remained to be said.

So much to be done.

To be done—my heart begins to pound.

All that everyone does. All that no one ever had done before.

All that I had already done.

Touched your elbow with my finger! All that remained to be done.

My chest will explode. What remains to be done? What is it I want to do? What can I possibly do? Let fly my soul like an arrow from your bow so it may soar free . . . somewhere . . . in its desire for death . . .

I turned sharply and almost knocked into her. Hey you! She steadied the tray.

Steaming hot chocolate and jeera biscuits.

And again as so many times before, she was in two places—inside me and in front of me!

72

The thing is, English, the language, and the story are alike in a way. Both are difficult, both are necessary, in the business of life. Not just 'business of life,' in 'life' itself, period. Not even *in* life, they *are* life!

Take English first. The New Yorker needs it as much as the native of the jungle and the village. What you have to do is, you have to summon it to yourself—the story, and English. One way of doing this is to memorize one phrase, for instance, 'come here'. Then you stand at one end and shout 'come here'. And when you want to make them return, run to the other end and shout again, 'come here'.

This is a tried and tested technique, so I can tell you its problems. One, you can become exhausted. Two, your breath can fail. You or your breath. It's a no win situation.

There is a better way though to understand that there is one end and then one more. Of a story or of life or of English. If you speak from this end, you are saying it now, but speak from the other, and you'll be saying it then. Say it then, and it is yet to be; say it now and it has been already. *Then* has wings and flight and hope, *now* lies crushed in the aftermath of the storm!

I wonder if you get what I'm saying. That in both cases The End has happened. Only the sequence changes. From one end the joy of possibilities, from the other, the counting of casualties. Ultimately of course, both are stories, imaginary, like life.

So shall I speak then or shall I speak now?

Then or now?

For if I speak then, when a new person had formed, whose heart had wings and love, wings and love, it would be a different story. I am I am I am in intoxication. Everything was joined to love and to the stars of loving desires. All the old fears, old flaws, old defeats, the soiled greyness everywhere, had bloomed green, yellow, red and pink in the newness of spring.

The empty space was real, around it the ashes of centuries. This is the real self. The rest, imprisonment. The fetters of religion, politics, faith.

Come like me, to that empty space. Then you may move on to anywhere else. Then you may become anything at all. Touch anything. Make your home anywhere. Soar, land, settle, not be trapped where history has placed you. Just gaze at the skies, keep gazing, till you see the empty space spread out between the birds and clouds and suns, till you realize that the sky is the empty space while the rest are just fragments distracting your vision, fragments of possibilities now complete, of erased lives.

Oh I'll speak *then* and not *now*! When every possibility still lay ahead.

When the preparations were on to send me away. To the well-known university in your state.

There were still a few months to go. Your work at Ma's institute was still carrying on. We keep meeting. See films. Visit friends. Ma says, *how he has opened up in your company.*

73

The day of your departure looms large. My heart sinks, but then in the very next moment it leaps up—I'll be there too, soon after.

Ever since you walked into my life this is how my heart has been—sinking, then leaping. Moody, like weather in the hills. My enchantress, you dance me to your melody when I gambol ahead, drown me in a trance when I fall behind.

You did not come yesterday. Today you will. You've never not come two days in a row.

Downstairs, Ma and Father must be waiting for you too. Ma's leafing through an old album. You've had it! She'll show it to you again. And you'll go through it as if you're thoroughly enjoying it. That's why we all adore you, you value our story as if it were your own. Each one is made to feel that no grief, no random moment is meaningless. Even the worst days are not worthless.

The way Ma has of bending over the stories in the album, unfolding them to you. Chattering away. The way you hold Father's hand, listening to him. I can't make out the words, but the intimate hum they spin wafts softly upstairs.

Where I wait, come on up, listen to *me.* I want to say, in brief, that . . .

But no, not briefly! In love, nothing can be briefly said. Ravenous, greedy, demanding love! All, all, all, I want it all. Stuff me full. Get it all and take it all.

Not a good thing, greed. After eating what you need, you swallow up what you mustn't.

Some day in my greed I'll drink you up. Oh, the bow of your eyebrows, one look at them, and anyone would be reduced to my condition!

But not just now. For the moment, vast desires are content to simmer quietly within little tremblings. To pat you lightly with a finger, for now that's enough. One day a thousand fingers will dance lightly over you. Become the rays of the sun playing on your body. One day I will reach the limits of my madness. I'll keep on talking to you, and you'll say, *is this it, you'll just keep talking?* And that's when I'll say, *don't touch me, I am fire.*

But now she has to leave. There will remain just me, and my loneliness. Uff.

I couldn't sit there any longer. Came downstairs. Ma, I'll just go out for a bit. Went outside. Started to jog. To sweat it out. Dreading the day the earth will turn back to earth and grass to grass with your departure. With you will go the spring that bounces me upwards, scraping my head against the sky each time my foot touches ground.

Say what you will, I shall be unhappy when you leave. Stopping my jogging, I want to tell you this. Do me this

kindness. Let me turn into a mosquito and come buzzing to your ear in all the languages of this world, and you will try to brush me off, but cannot, and I will say, you're going and I'm a little sad, *ka lim vak lo, thodu thodu dukh awe che, konjamm varuttamaa irrukku, thoda thoda dukh horya, naik burro lugyyohai, je suis un peu triste!*

Sad about so little, you will ask and I will ask you, so how much sadness should there be to make one happily unhappy? To which you will say . . .

Jogging at this time today? She asked.

I stood panting by the nala. Turned towards her. In that simple moment, our eyes met simply. Under the sky.

Have your eyes ever met someone's, under the sky, in a quiet undramatic way? That moment is sharply etched, like a drawing.

Under the vast sky, two specks of dust.

74

'Oh woe, you're leaving,' I said laughingly. 'Whom will I cry my heart out to now?' I complained. 'And my arched bow?' I flirted. 'All alone again.' I turned sad.

I had come to bid her goodbye at the guest house.

Tuk, she gave me a light rap. Rubbish, you're not alone! There's Ma, and Father . . .

Ma Father me. Me Ma Father. Father me Ma. My mind whirled.

'And him,' she looked towards the far end of the field.

I'd forgotten him! But no, he's always around somewhere. He's here, so we are! Can this back-and-forth of our presence–absence ever end? I call out absent, and I am marked present, I say present sir, and it is he who gets ticked present in the register!

Forgot him? She teased gently.

I was busy, *yaad karke yaad nahin kiya, par hum bhool gaye use, aisa bhi nahin.* Didn't exactly remember to remember him, but it's not as if I forgot him either.

You distracted me, I teased her back.

By now she knew everything. His turning into a legend posthumously, the story of which was recounted endlessly in my life.

'Come, shall we go there?' I asked.

Who knows why? Guilt because I sort of forgot him, or to push further the moment of parting? Or to please Ma that I cared to go light a lamp for him? Or to continue keeping this lovely girl joined to my personal story?

Who knows, who the hell knows? Whose wishes do we carry out when we do what we do? Our own or those of others before us?

'I'm surprised you never asked me earlier,' she said. Nor did you ever suggest it. I was equally surprised.

We had been doing so many things together, had developed a common routine in these last few months, would it have been so odd to do this together too? Maybe she had wanted to? Maybe she had been waiting for me to ask?

The field. Like a vast sky.

The crimson of the setting sun. In it, the circling of birds. The flapping of their wings, crimson.

Like her face.

The games light plays! I did not say it.

Closer and closer, the memorial crept up on us. It arrived.

There's a niche. Inside it are lamps, candles, matches, a duster, broom.

If he had been lying here, his feet would have rested here, here his head, looking up at the sky; but he could not lie down.

I dusted the marble. She wiped it clean. I lit a lamp. She lit a candle. Read his name on the plaque. And read out:

'Did he pick a flower?

He picked a hundred flowers. Did he smile?

He smiled a hundred smiles. Did he climb a tree?

He climbed a hundred trees. Did he see a star?

He saw a hundred stars.

Let us then go look for him, to say with love, he has returned.'

Together we arranged the potted plants around the memorial. Weeded them, watered them. Swept away the dry leaves and cleaned out the cobwebs.

You said bye-bye. I said, 'I'll come soon.'

But it's not in the saying that things happen. Nor even in the happening. What happens, happens in the quiet.

But only the memorial was quiet.

75

What remains to be told is only the story of the return. Return!

A short word with a million twists. Can't muster up half a smile but can wind round itself coil upon coil upon coil.

There was once a wise man. He said, 'You can never return. You can never step into the same stream twice. That neither is the water the same in which you dipped your feet the first time, nor your feet the same ones that dipped themselves then.'

The wise man said what he had to say. Those who wanted to believe, believed.

But listen, and listen well, to the wise one of this age— you can *only* return, all you can do is return. Whether the water is the same or not, whether we are the same or not, it keeps returning, that very moment, that very image, those very roots, that thirst, that empty space, that bomb blast!

But listen to this too, that the arrogant ones of this era never know that they are returning. They need to start from the same point each time all over again. They think that they march on ahead and that time is a dog on a leash, wagging its tail at their heels!

I tell you, every era has its pet words. This one's is—closure. People who like this word, hate the word 'return' for it opens up questions and more questions which close nothing. This era has no time for all that.

No time for questions such as these:

Was the return of the ball in its bounce when thrown, or in its being caught? Did the cloud return in its fullness or emptiness? Should the blown-out balloon be considered returned, or the shrunken one? And let me laughingly ask this serious question: when the meanings of words changed, did the meanings return or the words?

And when the boy shot out a bitter barb and the girl drew it into a sweet melody, what returned and when? And when the writer produced trash and the actor performed a masterpiece, what returned and when? And talking of trash, remember and try figuring out whether the son returned or trash, and when and where? And before the families of such sons tear me apart, let me throw up in the air one more question, that in the tales of Martin Guerre and Bhawal Sanyasi, in which the long-missing husband of the widow came back to the village, whom the village did not recognize, perhaps not even his widow, but they accepted him . . . at which point along the story will you place the word 'return'?

No, I'm not rambling, in fact it's only in the rambling that one can return. The lost, prodigal son wandered and returned home some two thousand years ago. The ten lost tribes of Israel are still returning to their homeland. Think of the amazing trajectories their wanderings took, from the races in Latin America to the Mongoloid races in Asia. Forgetting their language, history, ways and wealth, taking on the faces and features of the race in whose midst they lived—and now they return!

The world is enormous. From every corner expatriates and migrants, like ants in procession, are returning to their countries—from Australia and America to Europe, from the Caribbean to Asia and Africa, from the Rig Veda to the moon, and Pandits to Kashmir and the self-centred in modern designer garb and the foetus back to the womb and you to the heart and I to the which home . . . on the road . . . in the root . . .

For now one last thing. Everyone goes in order to return. But midway they freeze, wondering if the return would happen when they enter their house or when they step out on the road. So they freeze, rooted to the spot. And that's the search for roots!

So hold out your palm, open it, come on, and here, place on it what I tell you, like a pinch of tobacco and rub it, rub it fine, and whenever you are in a dilemma, sniff up a tiny bit—that return is possible but only to nowhere and nowhere is the only somewhere, for there are no roots anywhere, it is we who are rooted where we stand, speechless, wondering whether coming here is the return or going there?

76

I had to go, and the day for me to set out came at last.

I don't think it was discussed with anyone, but Father got into the cab too. It was a short flight, just an hour and a quarter, but it was barely daybreak, and so the house was turned upside down.

The way to airports is long. And everyone on it is going to the airport. Some to see people off, some to catch flights, some to make money. Air bags and suitcases peep out from cars. And the travellers are already dressed for the weather they are travelling to. That is to say, half their being is already at their destination, waiting for the other half to reach by flight!

Mine too. My very being is waiting for me at the other end. You have promised Ma you will take leave to come receive me at the airport and see me through the exams and things. Ma has made me promise that I will not go alone, but only with you, to that place I came from. I will hold your hand.

Right now it's Ma's hand I hold, sitting at the back in the cab. And when she holds my hand, streaks of light descend on the road, like someone is sweeping the darkness to the sides. Ma's face catches the light and she asks again whether I have checked everything—*ticket, money, her address, phone number, what if you overlook her in the crowd.*

Like I'd overlook her! But I don't joke like this with Ma. Nor like this, *yes, I've checked everything—spectacles, testicles, watch, wallet!*

But like this, I do joke—check *me* Ma, am I here?

Father says nothing on the way, and Ma says little. On such busy roads people often stash away their emotions, as if in their handbags, to open later at leisure and let them out hot and steamy. For now, the taxi, us, the airport, like parts of a machine, coming together in the routine of the moment.

So engrossed that nobody notices the butterfly that hovers over the bonnet. Flutters away, lands for a moment, then flutters away again.

But after a while, the road is so long, we begin to see it. That it flutters, then lands. This fragile little thing, will it come all the way with us? When it tires, it settles on the bonnet, then flutters away again. Rust-orange wings, black spots.

What else on the road to the airport? Gigantic signposts, gigantic lights, orange divider lamps in the centre of the road. As the airport draws near, planes start splicing the sky. We can see them, see the sky split in two, but there is no sound. But my heart begins to become a little active. For the first time, alone, away from home, true you'll be there, but that only makes it pound all the harder!

See, a butterfly! I show Ma. The cab will stop.

Ma says, finish the exam quickly and come back fast.

I laugh at 'quickly'. Okay, I'll press the fast-forward button, write it in half the time, and return!

Father is silent. He hasn't even smiled. Who had asked him to come? We will never know.

Fathers are strange. Haven't ever spoken to sons. Or combed their hair. Massaged their bodies. Held their hand, explained, teased, argued. Once in a while they say a few words to the air about something of importance to the world, but all the personal stuff gets left out, no?

The taxi stops. I jump out to fetch a trolley. I kiss Ma and she kisses me. Be careful, she says.

Fathers are strange. Sons must bend to touch their feet, and fathers must raise a hand in blessing, but the other one goes up too, involuntarily, into the void.

I walk quickly. Suddenly remembering the butterfly, I turn to look for it.

A flutter of rust and black, but as my eyes focus, it's not the butterfly. In my mind's eye that photograph surfaces, of him on his eighteenth birthday, in Ma's lap, a mug of beer frothing in his hand, cheers. His shirt is rust-orange spotted with black.

Father has forgotten to put down his arms. He's frozen in that pose, both arms held out, not like a father saying, go, my son, with my blessings, but like a tearful child wanting to be picked up . . .

My heart breaks.

I can't seem to push the trolley.

Someone shows me how to press the handle down in order to release the brake.

Is it possible I don't want to go?

It's as if I'm carrying on my back my own body that grows steadily more lifeless, its face turned towards

Ma and Father, and it's someone else who pushes the trolley along.

And that's how I set out on my journey.

77

I walked along, pushing the trolley, and the reluctant feet of the body on my back dragged on the ground, thud, thud, thud. The sort of sound one might imagine a trolley making if one of its nuts was loose.

'Why are you going,' the one on my back asked, looking backwards, where Father's upraised, pleading arms and Ma's sad face hung in the air, separated from their bodies.

But the one pushing the trolley ahead didn't care. After all, he was at the airport, the home of callous hearts and mechanized hospitality. Noise and order. The sound of machines whirring. Boxes on wheels and smart, ironed people. Between them meandering and zigzagging, long lines of trolleys joined to one another like bogies of a train, pushed along by airport staff. They were empty, mine had my box.

It wasn't *that* box! Still it went as freight through the X-ray scanner, jiggling on the conveyer belt like a skeleton. Images emerged on the monitor. What did the guards see? How far back and deep inside can X-rays pierce? Would I be stopped?

My gait uncertain, I walked past all the old entry points. People thought I was walking ahead, but I was dragging my reluctant partner-on-the-back along. I felt like I was being pulled backwards. Drag thump drag thump, about to trip and fall . . .

This going backwards? This going back to search? What are you looking for, brother? Yourself? Then where are you, sir? Here, or back there, or in the overstretched strings between here and there? Roots! In the search for the past . . .

Not just rooted, befuddled too. I watched with amazement as this backtracking gait of mine began to spread to other people at the airport, even the machines, like a contagious disease. They were all moving backwards. Or had my eyes turned around inside their sockets?

Thank you, I said to the airhostess and she too hurried backwards, escorting me to my seat.

The plane sped backwards on the runway. Quickly I pulled out the toffees Ma had stuffed in my pocket and sucked on them. The air pressure changes, she had said, and there will be a pounding in your ears, it can hurt, so suck and keep swallowing and you'll be fine, son.

The screen flashes the heights we're touching. Now thirty feet, now seven hundred and fifty feet, now thirty thousand.

Scared, I looked out. The plane was flying backwards, it seemed. Below us a floor of clouds, as solid as the earth. Or who knows, maybe the earth is as solid as clouds? Or . . .? It was the first time, in my memory, that I was flying. Naturally I was a bit scared.

A bird was fluttering just outside my window. The wings of the plane went whirr, and the bird spread its wings. Whirr, the air became a solid saucer, and the bird sat on it. Just a tiny creature, brain the size of a seed of grain, confident that it's flying on its own strength.

The plane kept flying backwards. The air hostess walked backwards, serving breakfast. My back—or somebody's—burdened with me—or with someone—kept going back, further and further . . . returning to write an exam.

Is this too called returning? When the back grows eyes to watch Father's pleading arms, while the face heads elsewhere, where it believes it will find itself, lying somewhere, like a coin dropped from a pocket, is that returning? All I'll need to do is pick it up and see if it's fake or not.

Yes, perhaps roots go back, back, back, searching, we keep searching, and totally lose ourselves! Here my roots are—but I, I'm not here!

So that's why I'm going—or returning—in order to deny that place from where I am not!

I am going, to burn down fully that empty space to which I don't belong, and complete the story and earn my release.

Flying backwards, then descending to earth, I will get off the plane. And because you will be there to meet me, for one special moment the fellow on my back will climb down and turn his face in the same direction as the one carrying him, and without any rivalry or push and pull, both, as one, will advance towards you.

You are the only one to whom I can turn entirely, without a split. Forwards or backwards.

78

When one reaches in darkness, towns appear neither familiar nor strange. In their glitter of lights, their high-rise buildings like plastic toys, their ambitions of becoming a world capital, each one appears the same. Security checkpoints, transparent trash bins . . .

Distinctiveness comes with the morning. At night, even a resident of the moon would find, on going back home, the same silver glow that's visible from the earth. Only morning will tell what it really is, and whether we belong here.

Okay, don't go to the moon, go somewhere closer, to another country, it's the same. I'm talking about those who for years and years, believed their roots to be in some country, guarding its precious image, like the moon, inside themselves. They finally reach it, and in the dark, they long to feel overjoyed, to feel, this is ours, this is us. But sometimes in the morning they realize that their roots are in the moon they have guarded inside themselves, the outside is but a strange land. Why did I return here? I must return there.

Oh all of you, desperate to return to your land of origin, beware, take heed, lest you should face the same fate. If you must return, why to that time, when you lay in that empty space in the stubbornness of the three-year-old? Why not to another time, before that?

But where?

Look, if you dare, for from round the corner of one of the lanes and footpaths and houses, suddenly *you* might appear. Want to come? Still want to return?

So if walking backwards has caught your fancy, why not return to any point in time. To any crossroads or curve. Why only into remote yesterday, go further back. Or walk forwards, why not? Or just slip quietly into today. If you so desire.

This game is about desire, not about roots.

But who thinks so much? When overwhelmed by desire? Who thinks at all, then?

Not I, at any rate. I push aside all questions and analysis and questioning. Out! All of you!

I just went along, towards wherever she was taking me. To a relative's place, who had gone somewhere and left the keys of his flat with her.

In the darkness of the car seat, lay our hands. Mine on my right and yours on your left. Between the two, the distance of a yard, in which unfolded the most enchanting stage of romance, its beginning. Yes, my beloved, wasn't that too an empty space, in which little starlights flickered? Invisible to the world, but their heat warming our hands.

But I knew nothing.

How could I know what was going to happen that night? Or it was the kind of thing that one always knows will happen

so that when it happens one recognizes it, but there's curiosity too. You know you will die, but when you do you don't know it, do you? Or like those prophets of doom who are always predicting the worst so that whenever some catastrophe takes place they can boast, see I told you so. But they never knew, really.

But what happened that night was no catastrophe. Nor death.

It was a magical night, the bow stringing the arrow, throb of drum and call of flute, tightness in my chest, my heartstrings stretching out and rolling back, stretching out and returning, the curled-up creature inside feverish, burning up. But I didn't know, when my chest tore open and it leapt out, whether it would pounce like a lion or purr like a kitten.

79

But if I speak *now* and not *then*? How would that be? What kind of human being would remain? One that has exhausted itself thrashing helplessly in a gummy swamp?

Even if I speak *now*, they would still be there, the words and actions, the sentences behind sentences and the faces behind the faces, that hovered always just beyond my seeing and just out of my hearing. If I speak *now,* all of that vast unseen and unheard is displayed before us, and I am outside the story.

Why should I think of this as mere coincidence? Outside the tale of the story! That's me, every time. With everything else that happens, the world weaves a pattern from it. It makes up its own stitches, weaves the tapestry it likes, and then patents it. So why should I be the only one, that whatever happens to me is meaningless, directionless, disconnected, just coincidence?

No, I protest. I too am destined! Not anybody's pawn, but marked by fate. This is what I am, a powerful text without a context. A rich, rich text without a context!

This is why I was created, to slip from the margins where I was, to the centre, only to find it was but an illusion, that I was always outside the story, that I remained outside. Lying in that empty space. That empty space my measure. Only that to which I can cry out, come embrace me.

Like that atom which collides into a field and begins to change its own nature. If a field of darkness, into that it submerges itself. If a field of light, it begins to glow. So happy that it expands.

Ecstatic! Its electrons fill with energy and it grows larger and larger. But then . . .

But then, sooner or later it must return to its old size. Return? Again? Unable to bear its own energy it must find

a way to release it? Through light, or through X-ray, somehow. Somehow it must spend itself.

This has to happen. With those like me. Born of the bomb. Caught in the confusion of these times. Again and again we must be left nowhere, belonging to no one, going through life, not belonging to it! Only one place is ever ours—that empty space.

If I speak *now* I can say a lot. When something is happening, it's happening, but when it has happened, you realize it was something else that had happened. Hearts had never met, nor eyes nor views, nothing was in sync. I imagined I was heading towards her, but she was on a journey towards herself.

When elders speak, it is not with remorse or self-pity, they cast pearls for the future. So listen to what I say—this is what is called contact, communication, touch, love talk, exchange, with life and the living. This approaching, hovering around each other, without ever really touching, whirling and swaying past each other, always missing the target, missed it yet again!

But just now the night is still young. Meaning *then*! The night was young. She said, come.

Into a magical space where she was alone and I was alone too. The town was the same one, where I hoped, the next morning I would spot myself running out from some lane to play marbles, looking as sweet, years ago, as I looked now with her. Out would bubble all the feelings of belonging that only a person of this town could feel. This is mine and I am its. We have known much grief but now we will be happy together.

The atom was expanding. You, my town, I. In all of this I will hear a word and remember my old language. Will see a fragment and piece together the whole picture. This town is incomplete without me and so are you. It seeks me for its completion and so do you. And gaining you and it, I will be complete.

This is why I'm here. All my wires exposed so that they may earth themselves, and glow with the electricity running through them. Unmindful that naked wires and electricity play other games too!

Longing to gather together my entire life in you, I followed you into the flat.

'Tomorrow will be a busy day, you must get some rest,' she said and left the room.

Is this what's called rest? You roaming in my mind, your voice echoing, your words wandering in me. You in the next room, you in my room, you outside me, you inside me. I feel giddy. This giddiness is rest?

You in every sound I hear. You, bathing. You emerging after a bath. You in the moist fragrance. The opening of the cupboard, the falling of the hanger, the dragging of furniture, are you calling me? Call. But you don't call. You will call. Won't you?

I couldn't stop myself.

I knock, I open the door.

You before me in the large mirror, eyes raised in mild surprise.

The boy saw the girl's hair unbound for the first time. Wavy. Drops of water. Poetry.

This poetry, it will never let go its clichéd imagery!

80

The boy comes into the room. The girl is seated, her damp hair spread on her shoulders like a poem.

Perhaps the boy cannot recognize the feelings rising in him? Nor does he know that such feelings have risen since the beginning of time? In that moment, all the passions smouldering like embers in eyes anywhere in the universe, burst into the room of the girl. An *oh* escapes the girl's lips, a sigh, an exclamation. And in the boy's mind arises the prayer: Oh God, spare me for a moment the knowledge of sin and redemption!

The girl gathers her tresses, ready to wind them up and jab a pin into them, as if it wasn't hair, but primal longings that had let themselves loose, and must be tightly leashed.

No. The boy forbids it. Eyes meeting eyes in the mirror. Frozen were the joined gazes and a ball of heat began to roam like a restless creature over limbs and bodies, threatening any moment to burst out, to plummet down, however steep the fall.

Such moments have come about since the beginning of time, when the eyes of the boy meet the eyes of the girl, and they are transfixed. The hunter, the prey, impossible to tell which is which. Unrelenting the mutual gaze, one blink and the prey might vanish or the hunter pounce.

The girl is seated on a stool, her back to the boy. But in the mirror she faces him. The girl on the stool begins to turn. With a gesture, the boy stops the girl in the mirror. She stops. The boy advances towards the mirror, their eyes locked in the gaze of hunter-and-hunted. The girl on the stool lets him go past her, closer to the girl in the mirror.

Close, so close the boy now, to the girl in the mirror that he can touch her if he touches the mirror.

The creature roaming his body has leapt into the forefinger of the boy. It rises towards the reflection. Towards the scattered tresses of the girl. Droplets on the strands. The tip of the finger alights on a drop in the mirror, like a butterfly. As if to slide it off. In her hair the girl on the stool feels a pull, and the drop falls. Like a glow-worm.

Keeps trickling down her forehead. Reaches the arch of the bow, and takes a little leap off it, right in the middle.

Challenges the fingertip, follow me.

The finger follows on the mirror. Running lightly down the nose, reaches the lips. The girl's head is trembling, and her lips part slightly against the touch of the finger. Like a kiss.

Oh! The voice of the girl on the stool quivers. What are you doing?

A choked sound escapes the boy, and the finger is still, filling itself with the softness of the lips in the mirror.

What are you doing? Now the girl's voice is a sob, and whether she is speaking to herself or to him, it doesn't matter.

Doesn't matter because in that moment a union is forming in which the boy and the girl both have become in themselves man and woman and wild animal.

Little sounds spark. The finger is sliding down the mirror. On to the body of the woman. Sketching it on the mirror. From lips to chin to neck, wherever the finger trails, there, a throbbing. Where the finger rests, the girl moves slightly, not to shake it off, but to lead it on.

Raised collarbones below the neck. In their hollows, a silver coin could rest.

The boy sketches a round coin there.

The finger slips on to the shoulder, to the line of her gown. It rests there, on the mirror, inciting the gown with its stillness. The pleading obstinacy of the boy's gaze blends into the eyes of the girl in the mirror, filling them with the intense blue of sky.

No. The girl wants to look stern but in the attempt, loses her balance further. Her restlessness makes the gown slip. Smooth curve of arm.

The finger on the curve, sliding the fabric down, down, down.

A fear, an intoxication, a hypnotic charge, blooms like a mist upon the mirror. Where a finger adorns a body as with henna.

You're so young, scolds the girl on the stool, but the girl in the mirror is only more aroused.

Is this right . . .? A drowning voice. In the mirror, eyes half-closed, faces melting, bodies trembling.

Finger on fluttering breast. Velvety. Intoxicating.

This isn't right . . .? Neck falling back, arms helplessly rising. The finger making love to every contour. Its touch searing with heat, only the reflection is real.

Don't, the girl's lie rings out, she gathers the folds of her gown at her navel, her eyes wild, the circling finger tracing the surface of her skin, losing itself in her lines, setting tiny pulse beats alight in her shadows.

The girl on the stool watches the finger drift over the marble body of the girl in the mirror. Watches, keeps watching. Moments joining on the glass, on open limbs. Nothing holds the finger back, nothing is forbidden, it draws everything to itself.

Irresistibly, the gown slips, and with it the finger, urgently seeking a centre . . . Like his finger, the boy slips too, and is on his knees, clinging to the mirror. The touch of his lips the offering of a devotee at the very centre of her being, at the fountainhead of creation and destruction.

No moment before this had ever been so long. No finger had felt so intensely before. Never a touch of lips like this touch, never again, never before; the very universe balanced on that fingertip, if it moved in the slightest, everything would collapse. Never ever, before or after, had such desire filled a mirror.

Wherever the finger had roamed, unrestrained, on the mirror, glistened the dewy outline of love and longing.

81

Because the moment the boy embraced the mirror, the girl sitting in it vanished.

I looked up to find in the mirror, only myself, my reflection.

Behind me, the girl on the stool moved in distress. I turned.

Her eyes terrified, seeking still that boy and girl of a moment ago, that man-woman-beast. Searching, she extended a finger, touched my lips, and when she drew it back, the rest of me clinging to her touch went hurtling towards her.

Drawing me with her, she fell to the ground by the stool. Shut her eyes tight. Holding something inside. I was whispering, touching her, trying still to be the boy of a moment ago, who had vanished when the reflection of the girl vanished.

Like the broken-off tail of a lizard we thrashed around for a little longer, that's all.

She shot up. Opened her eyes. What she had held inside them leapt out and ran away.

Only she remained and I. A cautious, mature, responsible girl, who will not let me be my age.

First we must talk. She said. Did I understand?

Now it's very late. I understood.

Tomorrow we'll go into town.

I understood nothing.

She got up, picked up the stool, picked me up, pulled up her gown, led me by the hand to the next room. Laid me down on the bed. Placed her hand on my forehead. Said, 'Go to sleep.' I fell asleep.

Like what happened was a dream.

Like I have come to the town-I-hear-is-mine from the airport, only to sleep at night and venture out in the morning in search of myself.

I woke up the same way. Allowing the crowd of questions to flock around me. Whose questions were they, the questions of how many, about who I am, where am I from, am I from here, is my past heavy and loaded, like his . . .?

He was also from here . . .

I thought of Ma. Wanting me to rake through the old ashes and retrieve a forlorn button. The soil she hates because it is soaked with the blood of her son, she wants me to kiss in reverence because it was the last to kiss him.

And somewhere here, who knows in what condition, lies too, my empty space . . .

We ate breakfast in the balcony.

Did something happen last night? Is that called the happening of something? Her face, composed. I gazed at it.

We got busy in other matters. Like we had been programmed. Roots, walls, writings, bombs, smart bombs, little boy, research your identity, draw together the wires, join them, become what you are, find out what that is. Find your connection!

We sat in the car. The town was still not my own, but nor did it feel like a tourist's destination, nor a pilgrimage. We were carrying on because that's why we had come. With eyes, ears, nose, all open, to let the town seep in if it will, or else remain a dot in the atlas.

Scrawled on the walls: *Spiders, lice and pests like that/Must be cleansed, no sin in that.*

The car gets caught in a procession, militant headbands, brandished weapons. The sort of procession one can see anywhere now. The kinds that set out on certain kinds of dates, certain festivals. Nothing to worry about, for a short while the traffic stops, for a short while on the other side of the glass, faces drunk with power, most of them eighteen or so, it's their day. Now they are a normal part of peaceful days too, so long as nothing flares up.

We drove on slowly, and when we stopped, before us was the university cooperative store.

Razzle dazzle. Goods galore. Red-painted walls. And on one side, opening on to the terrace, an enclosed area with plastic chairs and tables.

Here you get coffee. Hot and cold. She said.

This is what had become of that burnt out cafe of my childhood—a cafe now of the youth of others.

Yehi voh jagah hai . . . yahin par kahin aap humse mile the . . .

This is the very place . . . somewhere here it was, that you came to me . . .

82

Ek voh milna! Ek yeh milna!
A meeting, that. A meeting this, too. But oh the difference. She swept a look around, sat down at a table with me.

'Somewhere here, I was,' I laughed.

Like one laughs remembering the child of one's imagination, not oneself, really.

'And here he was, too,' she said.

'Yes, he too, somewhere here,' I said.

Did I understand? Nowhere around could I see anything to make it all seem real.

'Right here,' she said. Did I understand? No.

'In this place. Perhaps right at this table.' I did not, you see, understand, even then.

'Yes, exactly at this table.' She had said.

'Perhaps you were here too,' I had said. In that way of saying things, in the flow of a conversation, without really thinking about it, then realizing suddenly, that's exactly how it was.

'Yes, I was.' In that undramatic shop, in that undramatic coffee corner, looking undramatically at me, saying undramatically to me that yes, she was there.

Here!

'You could have told me,' I kept smiling. Did I understand?

'I did try to,' she said.

Yes, perhaps I understood a bit . . . not with a bang but with a whimper!

We quietly sipped our coffee. I reached out for the sugar, she moved the jar closer to me and left her hand near it.

I covered her hand with mine and said again, 'You could have told me.'

'You wouldn't let me,' she said.

'I did all the telling myself, didn't I?' I was still smiling, but I was not there, in my hand which was on hers.

'Yes, you did all the telling,' her eyes filled with tears.

I realized then, that here too, I had been just about to begin the telling. To recreate once again that pitiful emotion-filled scene. To make those eyes fill with tears.

Now I had lost that chance forever. How was I ever again, to make her listen, make her cry, win her love, be happy? I wish she'd waited a few days longer, let me tell her a little more, so much was left to tell. What could I ever say again, those tears would never flow for me.

The tears were already flowing, but I have a sudden flash of insight. Not at what *I'm* saying. That flash again. They had never flowed for me, not earlier, flash. Not now. Flash flash flash.

I dropped her hand. But started to feel so tearful myself, that I put my hand back on hers.

'You could have told me,' I patted her hand.

'You weren't ready to listen.'

Then I imagined a crazy scene. There she is, seated regally, goblet of wine in hand, and I'm gyrating to a cabaret number to seduce her, and all the while it's him she longs for, but I, unknowing, keep stupidly swaying sexily, and it is in this very cafe and he was here, and she was too, and I wasn't.

'When did you last come here?' I asked. Still a fool.

'After fifteen years, today,' she answered.

Did I catch on then? Yes, then I did understand.

'With him?' I asked. Or said.

'With him.'

'That day.' I said.

'That day.'

'When the bomb exploded?'

'When the bomb exploded.'

Her face was washed in tears. People had started to look at us. Then they left us to our privacy.

Had her face been so washed in tears for me ever? Ashes countering ashes, rising this way and that.

'I was sitting where I am now, and he, there, where you're sitting.' She said, looking at me.

Or at him.

83

Did this very coincidence have to happen?

Of course this very coincidence had to happen.

Don't get all confused about whose story it is—mine, not mine, his, not his, it's hers, the girl younger than him and older than me, no, it's Ma's, no Father's, or whose? Don't get lost. This is the story of the bomb in which everyone stands outside the story, except absence itself.

See, this is what I'm saying, that it's absence that races up and down people's veins. No bomb, no absence; no absence, no us. So this is what I'm trying to say . . .

But was I saying anything really? No. I was sitting quietly and she was doing the saying. All that she had been unable to say before, silenced by my obsessive she-knows-nothing-about-me babbling. Saying all of that now, what she was, what he was, and all that had happened between them.

He was her elder brother's friend. Not her brother really, some uncle's son. Not her uncle, but her father's best friend's son. During the vacations she would go to this brother-who-was-not-a-brother's house, and that's where she met him, where the two friends studied in the same school.

'They lived in your town.'

'Which town?'

'Ma and Father's.'

Which Ma Father? I swallowed the question.

'We were young.' She continued.

To my surprise a small shadow began to form beside her. Was it him or me?

'But you weren't three years old, were you?' I teased, patting her hand when she looked at me reproachfully.

She went on with the story. Of burgeoning innocent love. Their letters, their conversations, their aspirations, their growing intimacy, talk of his village, her hometown, his desire to come to it, the coming together of everything.

'I don't want to hide anything from you,' she said.

'Go on, go on,' I said expansively, generously.

'I went to receive him at the airport. For the first time we were alone.'

To stare unblinkingly into her eyes and listen attentively to her talk about someone else. That first moment of betrayal in which trust, out of sheer habit, was still spread out like a sheet.

'I knew,' she said, 'that everything would happen between us that day.'

You could have spared me a thought. At least the chance of being the first . . . But that was not to be. Nor my actually saying any of this.

She sat in front of me and the shadow beside her started to grow larger, would become eighteen, would experience with his beloved that moment in which everything comes together, all the senses would come alive in unison—smell, flavour, scene, skin, scream . . .

'Are you listening to what I'm saying, you're not listening to what I'm saying.'

Her tears, from another time, from another story, for another person.

My sheet of trust has ripped. From it peeps a three-year-old.

In my eye there forms just one, only one, splinter. A splinter of glass that hurt. But I was powerless to lift my hand and rub it away. The splinter slides inwards, hidden, descends into my body, through my nerves, bouncing along my veins, reaches my armpit where hair had begun to sprout and there's a manly smell. There it melts into a teardrop and keeps slipping down my side, to my waist, below my waist, down my thigh it went slipping. As it slips down, down inside my clothes, I can see it, hear it, feel it. And nothing else.

'We made love.'

'Tell me, tell me,' I say. Once the betrayal is over, all is leisure, the sheet was full of holes and from each rip, there's me, peeping.

I was looking at her and at the shadow growing sharper beside her, but she was looking at me and the same shadow was beside me.

84

Now she was speaking quite comfortably. It's only the first slap that's difficult to deal. The hand trembles, resists the impulse, the one who receives it goes into hysterics. But once that's done, it's easy. Both get used to it.

After that, she says, everything changed. He was always in her, with her, even when they were apart. Whether other men came her way, or not, he would remain. In her mind, in her body.

Such was their love. That if anybody else loved her, the old lover would leap in. Someone touches her, he would touch her too. Or sometimes he alone touched her, we other lovers standing aside politely.

Someone laughed behind me. I turned. Could have been anyone. So many people in that shop and coffee corner.

The university cooperative store was fresh and snazzy. Stationery, shuttle cocks, sanitary napkins, candles, toiletries, it had everything. Somewhere here had I been lying? Chuckling at the flying sparks, thinking they were fireworks? Did you hear?

Beyond the verandah, the road is visible. Someone is washing his car. Hosing it down, soaping it, directing jets of water, rubbing hard with a cloth, oh so ruthlessly, peeling off its skin, scratching it. A bunch of kids stands by, giggling. Perhaps it's their father's car. Perhaps I was one of them once!

It is unbelievable that from some lane of this very town had come a child holding someone's hand and walked into this cafe and no one noticed him? No one remembers him? For heaven's sake, if not for me, for your own security you should have noted carefully every face, every movement. At least you should have noticed whose finger it was that I came in holding, perhaps the other hand held a bomb?

She sat in front of me. Talking. Her face animated. Every inch of her animated.

She kept speaking, but what I began to hear was all that *I* had said to *her*. Every single thing I'd said, like a puffed-up balloon, gathered into a bunch in my hands as I sat before her. With every word of hers, a balloon of mine would burst. *Phuss, phuss,* one by one. I had thought I was telling her something new and unique and incredible, but she had known all along? Had she smiled quietly to herself?

This is a coffee corner but you could quickly grab some noodles too. Before going in to write the exam. Youngsters in jeans and shirts, laughing and talking. So much chatter and laughter . . . another balloon just went *phuss*!

I thought of giving her a kick under the table to shut her up. But what if my foot slides aside her salwar and caresses her ankle instead?

Like he must have done. Like I would never do.

I'll just continue to sit here. Where we had been sitting since then. Since the beginning.

'We were changed people when we came here,' she said.

Lucky fellow, he didn't have to hear any of this about someone else.

'Just once I want to tell you everything. Our bodies were singing when we came here.'

'Why did we come here?' I asked.

She gave a start. 'Because we wanted to.' Startled, she said, 'You . . .'

'And you?' I asked and didn't care whether there was an answer. This was everyone's pilgrimage. Ma's, mine, hers, his . . .

'You did not let me tell you,' she said.

'What?' I asked.

'Anything to do with him. You told me I was the first not to link you to him.'

I smiled. This woman was going to die. She was dying a little bit at a time, in front of me.

'And Ma also stopped me.'

Ma had known too. The son told his mother, Ma, there's a girl, she makes my heart burst with love. Then Ma loved that girl too, and warned her, that claimant who has come in his place, don't tell *him* anything. She said, he is weak of heart, protect him. Quarantined me from her son like I was infected, to protect him. Me him, him me!

Actually Father's way was the right way. No pretence of love, the shadow is the shadow, not the real. Father was right in his way with women. Partition them in slices, poke them in their folds, tear them with a finger like a knife, let them break, hurt, scatter, a bit and then a bit more, and let their bits make me a little whole, gesture authoritatively, here . . . undress . . . turn around . . . hang upside down . . . and give them nothing but those few inches that jut out, not touching me anywhere inside, to splinter, to explode, enjoying them only with those few inches.

'His last words were . . .' she picked up the coffee cup and raised it like a toast. But now it was herself to whom she was talking, and to the old cafe. 'To us . . . and . . . then . . .'

'The blast.' I said. Be quiet, I wanted to say. Before me she sat and I was missing her. Uff, how I was missing her!

85

She sits before me. Going on and on.

The shadow beside her was burgeoning into a giant. She sits in front of me. I'm missing her so.

She keeps speaking, wiping clean the lines I had written. Quiet, my soul was crying, quiet.

Her forehead had shrunk. I could see wrinkles on her neck. If you keep speaking nothing will remain. But I don't say

You should be quiet, I don't say, old stories say so. That a mother sent her daughter to fetch food and she brought back a duckling. What did the duck say, asked the mother. Nothing, said the daughter, it just turned and walked away. Then go back and return her child, said the mother. Who knows what lies behind the silence. It's dangerous. So the daughter returned the duckling and fetched a chick. What did the hen say, asked the mother. Raved and ranted, screamed and shouted, said the daughter. Fine then, said the mother, let's feast on the chick. When someone screams and shouts, there's nothing to fear.

She carried on talking. At her pilgrimage spot.

Here they had come, as one. He had raised the coffee cup. Cheers to us.

As she spoke, she raised my hand and touched it to her eyes.

There's not much difference between going on pilgrimage and doing black magic. They're just two ways of doing the same thing. In the first you say I am going to attain the Supreme. In the second you say I am going to exorcise the ghost. If you find God, the ghost disappears. If the ghost disappears, you find God.

If God is found.

If the ghost disappears.

But what am *I* in this ritual of God and ghost? The incense? The broom? With which the ghost is beaten out? Which is inhaled to achieve God?

'For years I didn't have the courage to face them,' she was saying.

'I stayed away, all those years. Like a culprit. I couldn't bring myself to carry to the parents the story of their son's death. But I kept track of everything that was going on with them.'

Kept track of every bit of news about the bomb family.

'Every time, I thought, how can I face them. But I also wanted to see you.'

Who has usurped his place, she wanted to see!

Why 'but' I wanted to see you? Am I to be defined always by 'but'?

'I mustered up the courage when I heard of the funeral. I wrote a letter telling them everything.'

So. Ma knew, this one knew, that one knew, *jaane na jaane gul hi na jaane, baagh toh sara jaane hai!* Only the flower remained all unknowing, the entire garden knew the state of affairs . . . I was being made a fool of, and I never knew. Deceiving myself that my chest was broader than it was, that my arms were wings, whirring away, flapping around the earth like it was the seventh heaven!

Ma and Father invited her home, embraced her with a thousand arms. She was, for them, not the witness to their son's death, but to his life. His partner in his last breath. In that cafe where everyone saw him dead, she had seen him alive, laughing and talking.

'We cried our hearts out when we met,' she said. Downstairs. Which I'd thought was only the transit lounge leading to the real story that would unfold upstairs. But it had never been that. I'd just imagined it that way.

She already knew all about my house when she asked me the way. Under that tree.

So the tree lied too? How far into the past can the lie stretch? Where can I return to find what was real? Here in this place? Somewhere here I was lying—that was me, was it not? This very me? Should I try to blow myself away and check? Or pinch myself . . .?

Suddenly with excruciating intensity I longed to belong to this town. Who was that three-year-old, from where did he come, whose was he? If I never know, it will be as if he never was, and then am I?

Or in reality did only he ever exist who was blown up, and like Govinda he entered every atom, so that wherever you look, there is He, there is only He. Govinda, you who belong to every *gopi*, to every Yashoda, you are their pain, you are their pleasure, it is you we all seek, if you are not, we are not.

She kept speaking, I kept going silent.

Inside me began to spread my silent town, to one side of which lay something obscure, which was growing fuller and fuller with the desire to roll into the middle and explode with a bang and cover everything this time, leaving no empty space, no me, no nothing. Oh bomb, don't reject me! Kill her, kill him, but me too—consider me as worthy of killing too!

'But honestly, I do like you . . .' she said, and something in my face made her lean desperately towards me.

But what she saw there made her recoil, stand up suddenly, her hunter-and-hunted eyes fixed on me, and looking at me still, she began to lower herself back, swaying a little, into her chair, but she missed, and slid down to the floor of the coffee corner, of that old cafe, descending like a celestial creature from the sky, falling from the heavens . . .

86

I sat like a murderer, waiting for a bang.

A bang. It used to be that a bang would scare children, but then they would see everyone laughing and be comforted. Oh, it's nothing, only fireworks at a wedding or a festival. Or it's the sky, merrily stretching out its belly, blowing rings of clouds through its nose and mouth, beating them like a tabla. The clouds burst with a bang, the reverberations reach the horizon, and lightning dances.

But now? Even the thundering of a cloud or the bursting of a paper packet makes people jump in fear, where's the bomb?

I kept sitting, drinking the coffee.

I could see her lying on the ground.

I kept seeing her hunter-and-hunted eyes. I kept wanting to kill her.

I kept longing for her.

I kept sitting, sipping my coffee.

Get up, my mind was saying, *give me a slap*. A hard slap. Spit on me. Humiliate me. Pick up whatever you can lay your hands on, this fork, this knife, and stick it in me so that the numb hurt inside me may come alive, bleed, ache, shriek. Just give me some simple physical wound that can make me cry, so I may have a reason to cry.

But why would she get up? Why would she do what I want her to?

I sat frozen, holding the cup. After all, what was so special about the story? The one she just told me? That she fell in love with her brother's friend and she still pines for her love.

Get up, so I can hit you. Get up and hit me.

Others had begun to shout. I sat quietly. Let them think how cruel, pitiless he is, there she lies and he makes no move to help her up.

People were running about. They were carrying someone wrapped in a blanket, by his hands and feet, a flaming body so hot that midway they let go, and he lay there burning like a sacrificial fire.

Many of those who were running were covered in blood.

I looked at the car outside that had been washed minutes ago. It had lost half its body. The remaining half completely charred. The driver a black statue, stuck in his seat.

Behind me, dismembered limbs and flesh.

Some part of a man or woman or animal was smeared on the wall—like an overripe fruit had been flung at it.

Blood in pink rivulets everywhere.

I had seen something like this before, a faint memory forms. It's called déjà vu.

Or a dream? Or reality?

Once in a city in India, in Poona, there was an English officer who narrowly escaped a bomb that exploded in his camp. His security officers came running, 'Let's move the camp.' The officer laughed calmly, 'This is now the safest place on earth, lightning doesn't strike the same place twice.' In the very next instant another bomb hit the camp and he was gone.

I would have laughed. Perhaps.

But at that moment there reached my ears a sound I had heard before, which I was hearing now. An explosion. Of a bomb. Of the second bomb.

The first time she had sat there, and he here. This time she sat there, I in his place.

I was intact. Once again. The bomb had gone past, leaving me untouched. *Useless. Reject him!*

The bomb was a sack of nitrate and nails. One nail flew straight into her heart and like a celestial being she descended from the skies to the ground, kept falling and falling . . .

What was it in my face that made her lean towards me? What was it in my face that made her recoil and stand up?

If she had not stood up at that moment, wouldn't the nail have flown past over her head?

87

What remains to be said after this? What had to happen, had to happen exactly as it did. I had to kill her and so I put on my face that expression which would place her in the path of the flying nail. And that nail had to pierce her heart.

In this way I turned her into the world's most beautiful beloved. Descending from the sky like an ethereal being and lying gracefully curved on the ground, taking with her forever the most exquisite, most fulfilling, most supreme possibilities of love.

With the living, love is always incomplete, hurt is inevitable. So I killed her.

What a stunningly lovely scene that was—the angel falling from the skies. Above those magnificent hunter-and-hunted eyes, that magical bow!

This picture will be endlessly repeated in the days to come, along with the news of the second explosion—all around, the commotion of the dying and in their midst, safe inside an invisible bubble, me sitting on a chair, she curving downwards.

The picture. I, sipping coffee. She, slipping to the floor. What will not appear in the picture is how after sitting rooted for a while, I put down the coffee. Carefully picked out the ashes and scraps of meat lying around me, and tying them into a bundle, began swinging the bundle from hand to hand, round and round, in growing anxiety about where I could fling it, where in the universe would I fling this bundle of the dead, because really, for how long would I have to remain attached to these dead, these departed, to this past, when would it be my turn, to know this is me, to experience something that was mine alone, something real, something unique, but I couldn't find it, I couldn't find a place to fling the sack.

So ever since then I have been searching, and maybe I need to find a place not for roots so much as for a mass grave.

I keep searching, and memories of you, the desire to talk to you, overwhelm me sometimes. So I come sit at this table, place you before me and start jabbering. Gradually I fall more and more silent, and then I go to Ma and Father, joining them in front of the television.

Because these days life really happens only on TV and those watching it grow increasingly lifeless.